WHIPLASH

Sandy Rivers and two fellow trail hands were taking a well-deserved rest in the Durant saloon when the injured man staggered to their table — whipped half to death, then knifed in the back. He had come to warn them of something — but died before he could finish what he had to say . . . The knife and lash-marks appear to implicate their old trail boss Amos Coyne; when he then steals the hands' horses, stranding all three men in Durant, there's nothing for it but to set out and track him down . . .

Books by Owen G. Irons
in the Linford Western Library:

THE DEVIL'S CANYON
THE DRIFTER'S REVENGE
GUNSMOKE MOUNTAIN
ON THE WAPITI RANGE
ROLLING THUNDER
THE BOUNTY KILLERS
SIX DAYS TO SUNDOWN
SADDLE TRAMPS
THE SHADOW RIDERS
RANSOM
LONG BLOWS THE NORTH WIND
THE HIGHWAYMEN
THE WAY STATION
THE HELLRAKERS
DERAILED
THE OUTLAW LIFE
THE PRISONER OF GUN HILL

OWEN G. IRONS

WHIPLASH

Complete and Unabridged

LINFORD
Leicester

First published in Great Britain in 2013 by
Robert Hale Limited
London

First Linford Edition
published 2015
by arrangement with
Robert Hale Limited
London

A catalogue record for this book is available
from the British Library.

ISBN 978–1–4448–2391–2

Published by
F. A. Thorpe (Publishing)
Anstey, Leicestershire

Set by Words & Graphics Ltd.
Anstey, Leicestershire
Printed and bound in Great Britain by
T. J. International Ltd., Padstow, Cornwall

This book is printed on acid-free paper

1

The saloon was pretty much silent except for the soft slap of playing cards meeting felt, the chinking sounds of poker chips being stacked or exchanged at the card table, and the muffled laughter at the bar where Jake Koons was sharing a private joke with the bartender, Pete Faber. Koons was a local gambler, a steady drinker who always seemed to have a smile on his face.

The quiet mood of the saloon suited Sandy Rivers just fine. The morning was still cool, and sharing a beer or two with the men seated at the round, red-painted table was almost like sleeping with his eyes open, much more welcome than the wild carousing that was expected of cowboys fresh off the trail could have been. None of them felt like celebrating in that way.

All three were still bone-tired. They

had been fired off the trail crew only the day before, and were plain weary. Not that they had been treated unfairly. The boss had made it clear that after the herd was delivered to trail's end, they would be let go. There was no need for them on the home ranch, the Sky Box which was located down near the Ruidoso corridor.

They had been hired on for the trail drive, had done their hot dusty work along the way, been paid for it and cut loose. It was the bargain they had made in the first place. With their pockets jingling with the silver from their pay they were making a pleasant, relaxing morning of it, each happy that they were not needed on the long ride homeward. Turk Bemis had put it best:

'Well, boys, we're trail-bums again, and for myself I couldn't be more pleased.'

Jerry Higgins hoisted his beer mug and said, 'Here's to spending the day sipping cool beer and not seeing the rear end of a single cow.'

The three Sky Box riders had agreed that it was time to enjoy a brief vacation. They had been bathed, shorn and shaved and had purchased some new duds without saddle holes in the seats of the pants. This was a moment of peace to be spent on an island of calm — the town had even been stocked with women, anticipating their arrival, but the cow hands were careful not to let one another give their trail wages to one of these prowling foxes with their innocent expressions and worldly experience, although they had lost Turk Bemis for a few hours the night before.

'No matter,' the burly Arkansawyer had told them early that morning, 'my jeans still jingle when I walk; it was worth having it once.'

Now the three men were content to sit and let the morning roll by with no work to attend to, with no plans for the murky future, without really having given a thought as to what tomorrow might bring. They had always managed, somehow, to make their way.

The red saloon door behind them opened on squeaking hinges. (Sandy thought someone must have gotten a bargain on red paint once, for every exposed wooden surface in the saloon was painted that color.) A man they knew from the Sky Box stumbled in, looking around frantically before his eyes settled on their table. He started their way. The man, whose name was Len Storch, had not been popular with the other hands. He had a face that reminded Sandy of what a bearded hawk might resemble: sharp nose and concave cheeks cluttered with a scraggly dark set of chin whiskers. He wore a battered hat and a faded red shirt with a torn shoulder seam — the same one he had worn all the way from Sky Box.

Jerry Higgins nudged Turk and all three of them looked toward the man in the open doorway.

Turk growled, 'If he wants me to hire on again, I'll flatten his beak for him.'

'Probably wants to try to borrow

4

some money from us,' Jerry Higgins said, turning his eyes down toward his beer mug as Storch shuffled toward them, boot leather scraping across the wooden floor.

'What is he, drunk?' Turk Bemis asked. For Storch seemed to be making heavy work of walking up to their table. He moved with the sort of bowlegged, uncertain gait peculiar to cowboys who have been living for weeks in the saddle. His boots dragged heavily.

Arriving at their table, Storch paused for breath as if he had been running to reach them. His eyes were wide; he held his right hand to his chest. When he spoke it was in a breathless, ragged tone of voice.

'I came to warn you . . . ' Storch said, and then he fell forward, his face glancing off the round table, his body hitting the floor with a heavy thud.

'Drunk as hell,' Turk said, from across the table, but Sandy and Jerry Higgins could both see the bone-handled knife sticking out of Storch's back.

'Looks like someone should have warned *him*,' Higgins said drily.

'What . . . ?' Turk asked, rising to his feet to take a better look. 'Well, I'll be damned,' he muttered after a minute or so. Len Storch lay still, sprawled against the saloon floor.

Higgins went to the man to crouch over him. Lifting his eyes he said, 'Doesn't look like he's going to get well, boys.' Higgins dusted off his hands and rose. The saloon had gone silent. The bartender and Jake Koons had broken off their conversation and they stared across the room in silence.

'Better get rid of him,' Turk said, taking a drink from his mug. Higgins glowered back and took his seat at the table again.

'I'm not going to do it,' Jerry Higgins said. 'Hell, I didn't even like the man.'

'I didn't like him either,' Turk Bemis said, growing surly. 'And he still owes me two dollars!'

Pete Faber spoke up from his position behind the bar. 'I didn't even know the man,' the bartender said, 'but I'd appreciate it if one of you would like him just long enough to remove him from my premises — it ain't good for business to leave corpses lying around in here.'

Grumbling, Turk rose from his seat. Jerry Higgins was looking away pointedly, his arms crossed. 'What makes it my problem?'

There was nothing else for it. Sandy Rivers sighed and stood.

'Let's put him outside at least,' he said to Turk. 'We'll figure out what we're going to do with him later.'

'Around here, it's customary to bury a man in his condition,' Jake Koons said from his place at the bar.

'I'm not burying the bastard,' Jerry Higgins grumbled.

'Then we'll find someone and pay a few bucks to have the job done,' Sandy Rivers said. 'Come on, Turk — grab an ankle!'

'You can take him out the back way,' Pete Faber said, nodding that way. 'No sense scaring off customers before they even get in the door.'

Sandy crouched down and struggled to remove the deeply embedded bone-handled knife from Storch's back. 'What are you bothering with that for?' Turk asked.

'Doesn't seem fittin' to drag him on his face,' Sandy said. 'Roll him over.' He looked at the bloody knife in his hand thoughtfully. 'Doesn't this look familiar to you?' He offered the knife to Turk's view. Scowling, Turk Bemis examined the weapon.

'I've seen a few like it,' he said, handing it back to Sandy Rivers, who tucked it away in the pocket of his leather vest. 'Why? You think you know who it belongs to?'

'Amos Coyne had one like it. I saw him cutting his meat with it one day on the trail.'

'Coyne? Why would the trail boss kill Storch now, after putting up with him all along the trail? Coyne's already paid us off and ridden south with the home crew. It's another knife like the one Coyne was carrying, that's all.'

'I suppose, but did you get a closer look at Storch's back? His shirt's torn to ribbons. He's been whipped. There's only one man we know who carries a bull-whip — Amos Coyne.'

Coyne had no real use for the long braided whip he carried coiled in his hand. On the ride north he had used it more frequently than was necessary to snap the flank of a steer that was moving too slowly to suit him. It had seemed quite unnecessary to Sandy Rivers. All that was needed to keep the steers moving was the nudge of a cow pony's shoulder, or the occasional slap of a coiled rope against their butts, but Coyle had enjoyed his sport, it seemed, and after all, he was the trail boss. If he wanted to amuse himself like that, it was no one's business.

'Storch is dead; Coyne is gone, Sandy — it's none of our business,' Turk said. 'Let's get him out of here and get back to our beer.'

The bartender was holding a side door open for them and they dragged Storch across the room by his ankles and through a storeroom stacked with beer barrels out into the sun-bright alley behind the saloon.

'He's heavier than he looked,' Turk Bemis said, straightening up to take a deep breath of the dry air. Dust drifted on a light breeze. The leaves of a trio of cottonwood trees opposite fluttered in the wind. A crow rose from the trees and flew away, cawing with censure, its morning peace having been disturbed.

'Well,' Turk said, standing with his hands on his heavy hips. 'We got him out. Now let's get back inside where it's still cool.'

Sandy Rivers tilted his hat back and squinted along the alleyway. 'Nope,' the younger man said. 'We've got to bury him, Turk.'

'Why've we got to bury him?' Turk asked unhappily, thinking of the beer he had left on the saloon table.

'He was our trail mate,' Sandy said,

shaking his head. Briefly he removed his new pearl Stetson to wipe back his pale hair. 'And he was a man. We can't leave him out here for town dogs and varmints to get at. Check that shed over there. They'll have shovels used to bury their garbage. I'll drag him up nearer the trees.'

Grumbling, Turk started toward the shed attached to the back wall of the saloon. There was a hasp for a lock, but on this morning, the lock had not been snapped in place. Reaching inside the flimsy shed, which seemed to be a place for black-widow spiders to congregate, Turk removed a shovel and a pick and returned.

'And me in my new clothes,' Turk complained, handing the shovel to Sandy.

'He'd have done the same for us,' Sandy Rivers said, nodding at the dead body, which was already drawing bluebottles.

'You think so, do you?' Turk growled. 'Name me one thing Storch ever did for

11

anyone all the time we knew him.' The pick Turk was wielding arced through the air, flashing dully in the sunlight.

'He used his last bit of strength to come and warn us,' Sandy said, squatting on his heels, waiting for Turk to loosen enough dirt to shovel.

'Warn us!' Turk stopped his motion. 'Warn us about what? Rustlers, Indians, rattlesnakes?'

'I don't know,' Sandy had to admit, 'but he was trying to do something for us.'

'He had only gone berserk from the loss of blood,' Turk said, stepping aside so that Sandy could use his shovel. The ground was hard-packed on the surface, but mostly sand underneath with only a few rocks.

Another half an hour and they had a trench dug that was deep enough for their purpose. They rolled Storch into the grave and covered it up again. 'Why'd this have to happen just when I got myself a new set of clothes?' Turk grumbled. He was trying to dust off the black trousers he had purchased only the day before.

'There's a lady at the laundry down the street,' Sandy told him. 'She can probably sponge them off real nice.'

'They still won't be new no more,' Turk said almost sadly. 'Things are only new once, Sandy.'

'Come on,' Sandy said, throwing an arm across the big man's shoulders. 'Let's get back to what we were doing.'

They replaced the tools in the dilapidated shed and entered the saloon again, to find Jerry Higgins still at the table, sipping from a fresh mug of beer. Sandy Rivers sat at the table, dusting his hands off. He had borrowed a bar towel from Pete Faber on his way in, but his hands still felt dirty. Turk had ambled toward the bar and grabbed them two new beers. Jerry Higgins had drunk their last two. 'No sense letting them go flat and warm,' he had told them. Neither of his trail-partners bothered to make a comment.

As they lingered over their drinks the

door opened and admitted two chattering bar girls. Minutes later another two colorfully frocked saloon girls followed.

'Must be time for the evening rush,' Turk observed.

'Which one was yours?' Jerry Higgins asked. 'I mean last night? I never did get a good look at her.'

Turk looked the women over as they gathered near the bar to speak to the bartender. He scowled. 'To tell you the truth, I never did get a good look at her face myself. Besides, she's probably still resting up. She'd need it.' Turk grinned, tilted back in his chair, took a hefty gulp of beer and looked across the table at Sandy, who was deep in thought.

'Are you still thinking about the grave?' Turk asked.

'Not so much — I've seen my share of graves. It's the warning I was thinking about. What did Storch come to warn us about? It was important enough for him to walk here with a knife in his back.'

'I told you before — he was

14

half-crazy from lack of blood,' Turk said. 'It doesn't matter anymore.'

'It might,' Sandy said unhappily. As the evening saloon crowd began to drift in, attaching themselves first to their drinks and then to the girls, Sandy shifted uneasily in his chair, wanting to be away from another stormy night. He was not cut out for rowdy drinking. Nor did he get paid enough to support such revelry. Finally, he slapped his empty mug down on the table and told the others, 'I believe I'll go along to the stable and check on my horse. Anyone want to come along?'

'Let's just stay for a while and see what kind of excitement we come across,' Jerry Higgins said. He was obviously getting a little drunk, having been seated at the table in front of a constant flow of beer most of the day.

'Turk?'

'I think I'll stay here for a while longer myself. I might run into something interesting. Hell, I've seen horses, Sandy.'

'Do as you like then,' Sandy said, rising. He replaced the chair at the table. 'I mean to ride out of town with something left in my pockets.' Turk, he saw, already had bleary eyes fixed on one of the saloon quail. Jerry continued to see only the bottom of his beer mug. He was not going to easily convince those two to move. Well, it was their life, their night, their money to spend as they wished.

The door to the saloon was opened by a wide-shouldered man in a red flannel shirt as Sandy approached it. This one had plans too; he already smelled of whiskey and reeked of bay rum. Sandy edged past him, through the door and out onto the plankwalk in front of the saloon. The late afternoon sun was directly in his eyes, momentarily stunning him as he began walking up the street, finding that he was tottering a little. The stable was three blocks along the street on the opposite side. Durant Stable was prominently painted across its sun-faded face in four-foot high white letters.

Durant, Colorado was the name of the town in which they found themselves. Every third building had the name 'Durant' attached to it — Durant Hotel, Durant Saddlery, Durant Dry Goods Store. Sandy had no idea who Durant was or had been, but the man had swung a wide loop.

Sandy crossed the street after first letting a buggy with an older couple riding in it pass. The scent of cattle was still heavy in the air although the stock pens had been cleared of beef the morning before.

Durant was on no regular railroad line. It was a spur built to accommodate the cattle trade, and the trains only ran as requested. Many of the ranchers in Colorado and Utah found the arduous drive to the Kansas trailheads too time-consuming and too risky, so they welcomed the Durant spur. Of course, arriving too early or too late could leave a rancher with a herd of beef standing in the pens devouring feed at a costly rate. Still, Vincent Skye, owner of the Sky Box Ranch, welcomed the convenience. He was able to get a much more rapid turnover for his beef. And, being much nearer, his cattle still carried a better weight than those that had to be driven through to Kansas.

Sandy Rivers entered the shadows of the Durant Stable and looked around for his horse. It was a strapping gray with three white stockings and a splash of white on its chest. It couldn't make the fancy moves of the cutting horses that Turk Bemis and Jerry Higgins rode, but it got him to where he was going without complaint.

Lazily a man appeared from the back of the barn scratching his head and yawning. He wore tattered overalls and had a greasy head of lank dark hair.

'Help you?' he asked.

'I just wanted to see to my gray.' Getting a blank look, Sandy expanded his description of the animal. 'Big animal. Three white stockings.'

A light dawned slowly in the

stablehand's eyes. 'Sky Box horse? I had to have somebody explain that brand to me! You would never guess — '

'Yes,' Sandy interrupted. He had spent much time explaining the Sky Box brand to others. What it was, was an empty square with three loops across the top indicating clouds. Vincent Skye had designed it, and it was one brand that was almost impossible to alter. That was neither here nor there. 'Can you tell me where my horse is?'

'If it was Sky Box, it's gone,' the stableman said, yawning again.

'What are you talking about? That was my horse and I left it here for you to watch!'

'Can't help it,' the man said truculently. 'The trail boss — Coyle . . . ?'

'Coyne. Amos Coyne.'

'That's the man. He came by and said any horse that was wearing a Sky Box brand was to be handed over to him. Your pony's gone, friend, along with any others that were left behind.'

2

'What do you mean our horses are gone!' Turk Bemis bellowed. He was sitting on the bed when Sandy delivered the bad news to their hotel room. He rose and moved to the window to peer out. He now moved with a noticeable limp, Sandy noticed.

'Just that — there's no other way to put it,' Rivers replied.

'Took my horse?' Jerry Higgins moaned. He was sitting in a wooden chair in the corner of the room, his head buried in his hands, the obvious victim of too much of the free-flowing alcohol in the saloon. 'Who would steal my little pony? I'll have his scalp when I catch him.'

'How are you going to catch him?' Turk asked roughly. 'Trot after him?' Then he turned toward Sandy again. 'Are you sure it was Amos Coyne who took them?'

'The stableman was sure.'

'The dirty dog,' Turk muttered. Sandy saw the big man's fists clench tightly. Turk rapped one of them against the window frame. 'So what are we to do now?'

'What can we do?' Jerry Higgins asked, peering through his fingers with bloodshot eyes. 'We get us some horses and ride the man down!' he said explosively. Apparently that outburst was enough to start his head throbbing again, for he tightened his grip on his head.

'I don't know a good place to get free horses,' Turk mumbled, 'do you?'

'Why we can just . . .' Jerry's thought trailed off, as the full import of their situation settled over him. 'Haven't you got any money left, Turk?'

'No more than you,' Turk Bemis grumbled. He took the new Stetson from his head and eyeballed it with distaste. 'Wasted most of it on my new duds, it seems.'

'Yes, and you went to visit that girl

again, didn't you?' Jerry Higgins said accusingly. 'I told you to watch your wallet better.'

'At least I have something to remember,' Turk shot back. 'All you've got to show for your pay is a roaring headache.'

'This won't get us anywhere,' Sandy Rivers told them. 'There's no point in bickering. Nobody did anything wrong except spend his coin as he saw fit. The question remains — what are we going to do now?'

'I don't see how we can do much of anything,' Turk said, stamping back to the middle of the room in heavy steps.

'Maybe not,' Sandy said. 'Let's try to figure a way.'

The other two trail hands looked hopefully at their youngest partner. Sandy had his pearl-gray Stetson tilted back on his head so that his cornsilk-colored hair fell free across his forehead. He said, 'How much money have we all together, boys? Empty your pockets and toss the coin on the bed. We're in this together; we might as well pool our funds.' Slowly, almost painfully, Jerry and Turk dug into their pockets and tossed what they had onto the blue bedspread. There was a lot of copper, some silver and the rare glint of a gold piece. 'We owe the hotel some money,' Turk said as Sandy set about counting up the cash. 'Four dollars, I think.'

'That's the least of our worries,' Sandy said, frowning at the scant amount of money they had among them.

'That sure isn't enough for three horses, three saddles and tack, trail supplies and saddle gear — canteens and such,' Turk said.

'Not even close,' Sandy agreed. 'It might almost be enough to outfit a single man if he didn't care what kind of plug he was mounted on and was willing to eat nothing but beans and rice for a week or so.'

'That would leave the other two men stranded and stone broke,' Jerry Higgins pointed out.

'Instead of three,' Turk commented. 'That cash will be gone in a few days and then we'll have nothing at all anyway. I say let one of us ride after Coyne. The other two can maybe find some kind of work in Durant — enough to survive on. Mucking out the stables, sweeping the saloon floor . . . whatever is available.'

'And if there isn't any work to be found?' Jerry Higgins asked.

'Then they'll be sad pups, won't they?'

Jerry thought for a moment in silence. Finally he looked up and said, 'I need a drink.'

'You can't afford one!' Turk shot back. 'That's a part of what got us into this mess.'

'Don't you be blaming me,' Jerry Higgins complained. 'I saw you and that skirt, and I told you — '

'Shut up,' Turk said heavily, and Jerry went back to holding his head, rocking from side to side in the hotel room chair. Turk turned thoughtful again.

Finally he sighed, shrugged and said, 'I say we outfit the kid as well as we can and send him after Coyne.'

Now in his mid-twenties with five years working alongside Turk and Jerry, Sandy bristled slightly at still being called 'kid', but the term wasn't enough to get upset about, especially in their present circumstances.

'Why him?' Jerry demanded.

'He's youngest and probably strongest. He threw the most money into the pot. He knows the trail better than anyone I know. And,' Turk said a little roughly, 'you and me are the sinners here, Jerry. We should have watched our pennies a little better.'

'I told you — ' Jerry Higgins began. Turk cut him off.

'Let's not start that up again. Do you feel like riding today, Jerry?'

'Maybe next week,' Jerry Higgins said, unhappily wagging his tortured head.

'Let's just go with my plan,' Turk said. 'Unless you happen to have a better one.'

'I don't.'

'Then, let's let Sandy see what he can do about outfitting himself. We'll get by somehow — we always have.'

Jerry shook his head as if he had grave doubts about that, but he only watched in silence as Sandy Rivers scraped the coins from the bed into his rawhide purse, mentally counting the money again as he did so. Sandy's face was creased with concern.

'Just do the best you can, Sandy,' Turk told him, placing his heavy hand on Sandy's shoulder. 'I'm sorry to even have to give you this job. You're going to be riding rough for awhile.'

'It doesn't matter,' Sandy said, tucking the money away. 'I'll pay the price for a few days, but when I catch up with Coyne, I'll make sure that he pays more.'

At the doorway Sandy shook Turk's hand. When it came to be Jerry Higgins's turn, Sandy passed a fifty-cent piece to the Arkansas wrangler. Jerry looked at him with surprise. 'That much won't make much difference to me,' Sandy said in a low voice. 'Try to get yourself well.'

★   ★   ★

It was a rat's scheme that Amos Coyne had devised. The question was, why had he done it? Their three ponies and their gear were worth some money, but did the trail boss need it that much? He was risking his job, of course; if Vince Skye ever found about it, Coyne himself would be on the receiving end of the whiplashes. Maybe the trio of abandoned men weren't worth that much to the ranch owner, but his reputation was important to him. Try to hire on extra men for a trail drive when they knew that they might be deserted and left afoot at the end of it.

A man with a good horse and a gun alone in the broad expanse of the West was one of the noblest men on earth, among the freest; a man alone and left afoot on the wide land was nothing at all except buzzard bait.

Sandy Rivers went looking for a horse.

The obvious place to begin was at the Durant Stable, and so he started in that direction. Sandy found himself wishing that his friends had been a little more watchful where their money was concerned. But how could he fault them? They had spent a month and a half on the trail, most of it along broken trails and not across easy flat land. Keeping the cattle bunched and moving was pure torture under a hot sun. And, there was no time away from the job — it was a twenty-four hour a day job. When the cattle were finally penned and ready for shipping, the men took it as their right and their due to celebrate as hard and as long as they could.

It was no way to accumulate wealth.

The tall twin doors of the stable stood open wide as Sandy crossed the dusty street. Behind the building there was a corral where an assortment of horses stood. Some sleepy-eyed, some bright and eager. Sturdy or lean-appearing, Sandy did not see a plug among them. His hopes rose.

When he entered the shadows of the horse-smelling stable, curious animals lifted their heads to observe him. There were some beautiful animals among them, but these would be owned by well-heeled local citizens or traveling men with resources. The best of the animals were kept sheltered and near at hand. The ones in the outside pens could have come from anywhere — abandoned or strayed, perhaps stolen. Sandy didn't bother to call out to announce himself. Stable managers were quite aware of any comings and goings in their pungent kingdoms.

'Help you?' the man with the lanky frame and ill-fitting overalls asked, coming toward Sandy, wiping his hands on a red rag.

'I hope so,' Sandy said, trying to put some cheerfulness in his voice. 'I find myself afoot and I need a horse and gear.'

'Bottom to top?' the thin man squinted at Sandy. 'You didn't even keep your saddle?'

Sandy refrained from reminding the stablehand that he had given horse and saddle away to Amos Coyne. He just replied, 'I'm afoot and don't wish to be.'

'Spent all your coin over at the saloon, did you?' the man said with a broken-toothed grin.

'Something like that,' Sandy answered. It was no time to explain; there was no point in it.

'A saddle, I don't know,' the stable-man said, scratching at his greasy hair. 'I've got a fancy fifty-dollar rig left by some gambler who got himself shot over a busted flush. After that, well, I've got a broke-down army McClellan saddle with the wood frame poking through the leather. It ain't worth fifty cents, but I'd sell it to you for five dollars if you're that need-ful.'

'I'm that needful,' Sandy had to say. 'How about something to throw it over?'

'Well, let's get down to it, friend. I'm

not in a dickering mood. How much exactly have you got to spend?'

Sandy told him, displaying the carefully counted coins. The stablehand frowned and scratched his head again. 'And you're shopping for a real live animal?'

Sandy didn't react to the sarcasm. He stood with the handful of coins glittering in his outstretched hand. It was a pathetically small amount: still, Sandy could see the faint glimmer of greed in the man's dark eyes.

'I might fix you up,' the stablehand said. 'Are you planning on riding far?'

'I'm hoping not to, but there's no telling.' The stablehand had started toward the outer door and Sandy fell in beside him, his confidence sagging. The first sight of the horse the man had in mind to sell him did little to lift that confidence.

The buckskin horse was shaggy, its legs stumpy and more like those of a plow horse than a cow pony. Its eyes were dull, its belly sagged. It was somewhere on the far side of twelve years old, Sandy guessed.

'I can let you have him cheap,' Sandy was told, as the two men stood side by side with their boots on the lowest rail of the pole corral. 'I can't seem to find a buyer for him.'

'I would guess not,' Sandy said. 'Have you anything else?'

'In your price range?' The man didn't burst into laughter exactly, but he shook his head, holding a chuckle in. 'Sorry, son, this is the best — no, it's all — I can do for you.'

'Throw in bridle and bit?' Sandy asked.

'I suppose so,' the stablehand said reluctantly. 'Listen, friend, if it breaks down on you, don't bring him back here, will you?'

'No,' Sandy answered as they started back toward the stable. If the shaggy buckskin broke down on him along the trail, he would be in no position to take the old horse anywhere. Nor himself.

The rest of the day was a long

process of haggling over a few pennies. He managed to find two battered, used canteens at the dry goods store where the salesman sold them to him with a look of pity on his long face. Food was more of a problem. He had earlier told Turk and Jerry Higgins that they could afford enough for beans and rice, but that would mean taking a kettle along to cook in and wasting hours letting the food boil. He was not willing to do that.

There would be some game along the way, but neither his Colt nor his long gun was the proper tool for popping rabbits. There was plenty of deer in the area, but that would mean taking the time to butcher one out. Sandy thought that time was one ally he did not have.

He instead filled a sack with parched Indian corn and a wide paddle of beef jerky, then waited while a cook at one of the local eateries deep-fried a batch of corn dodgers for him. He was going to be traveling hard. His anger against Amos Coyne built throughout the day as he made his small preparations.

Finally returning to the hotel on the back of his preposterous mount, he was unsurprised to find that Turk and Jerry Higgins had checked out. 'Try the saloon,' the bald, red-faced clerk advised him. 'That's where the down-and-out trailsmen usually head first, isn't it?'

'Yes,' Sandy muttered, 'it seems so.' He started that way, reluctantly leading the buckskin which drew a few glances and more than a few snickers. He had passed fifty cents on to Jerry just to combat his hangover, but even drinking nickel beer, his partners must be dead broke by now.

When he again entered the saloon it was to find his two friends at the very table where they had wasted most of the day. Sandy closed the red door behind him and walked to the table, glancing around. There was a lot of mostly good-natured bantering going on. The saloon girls laughed uproariously at any faintly amusing comment the men made. Pete Faber dutifully served up drinks. His waxed black mustache twitched as he smiled back at the half-drunk saloon patrons. He was good at his job.

'Look what dragged itself back,' Jerry Higgins said, as Sandy Rivers seated himself at the table. Each of the other two had a beer mug in front of him. They had managed to stretch that fifty cents out pretty well, it seemed. Jerry's eyes were glazed again. Sandy could guess which of the two had done the most damage to the half-dollar. He supposed there was no point in mercifully trying to sober up someone who did not wish to be sober.

'Have any luck?' Turk Bemis asked seriously.

'Well I've got a horse and saddle — they're nothing to brag about.'

'Got any money left over?' Jerry asked, and Sandy just shook his head. Whatever he had in his pocket which couldn't be much more than a dollar or so, he might need along the trail. Turk gave him an understanding look.

'This is as bad as being back on Sky

Box,' Jerry said, pulling his hat lower down on his forehead.

What he meant was that Vince Skye did not allow liquor on the premises and he kept a close rein on his cowboys, allowing them only limited access to town and its allures. You couldn't blame Skye — he was trying to run a cattle ranch, not a social club.

'No, it's not as bad,' Turk commented. 'It's worse. At Sky Box you always had a horse, and you knew where your next meal was coming from.'

'Did you find a place to sleep tonight?' Sandy wanted to know.

'Yeah. Pete Faber said he remembers well the times when he was in worse shape than us. He says we can drop our blankets on the floor of his storeroom at least for tonight. He's not such a bad guy.'

'Did he say anything about giving you boys a job?'

'No.' Turk shook his head. 'I'm not sure he's got anything to offer, but tomorrow we can start looking around town for something to do.

'What do you think, Sandy, is there any chance you can catch up with Amos Coyne?'

'I'm hoping so. He'll have to stop to cook and eat, to sleep. I don't plan on doing much of any of those things. I just hope that nag I'm riding can give me a few good days of trail time.'

'Can we take a look at the horse?' Jerry asked.

'It wouldn't be worth your while,' Sandy said seriously. 'All I can say about it is that it's got four legs.'

'Have you got plenty of food and ammunition?' Turk asked, his dark eyes growing darker.

'I have plenty of ammunition,' Sandy told him, rising from the table.

'When do you plan on leaving?' Jerry asked. Sandy glanced toward the windows of the saloon.

'There's still a little sunlight,' he answered, 'I've got nothing to wait around for.'

3

Passing through the deep shadows cast by the buildings along Main Street, Sandy rode the inelegant buckskin horse out onto the wide desert. Daylight was rapidly fading. The skies behind him were a wash of purple and dull red. There was already a nightchill in the air. The horse stumbled more than trod forward beneath him. He wondered if the old animal was dozing on its feet.

Within an hour there was no light except for a few faintly flickering stars above him and the distant feeble lanterns in the town he had left. The land rose up and grew rockier. Sandy knew where he was — at least roughly. He had ridden this trail a time or two, but that didn't make it simpler to traverse in this light with a swaying, staggering horse beneath him. The

McClellan saddle jabbed at him and rubbed him uncomfortably. He wondered if General George McClellan had hated his men that much.

That was unfair, of course. It had been wartime and the general had been trying to design a cheaper, more easily mass-produced saddle for his cavalry corps. All the same, Sandy would have bet that the general had never sat one of the wooden-framed instruments of torture himself. The saddle and probably the buckskin horse must have been ridden by an ex-soldier who had come West and given it up or had died.

Sandy let the aged horse find its own way up a low knoll, weaving along its path. The old animal was willing; it was doing the best it could, but it was just not good enough. Not good enough to have a prayer of catching up with a well-mounted man with a long head start.

At the top of the knoll Sandy reined in the buckskin, allowing it to catch its wind. Pushing the horse beyond its limited endurance was going to do him no good at all. Sandy's original idea had been to ride on through the night when any other man would be sleeping, thereby closing ground. However, the horse he sat had already indicated it was not up to a night ride. What now?

Just plod on and hope to make it as far as they could while the silver stars grew brighter against the inky sky. The moon, Sandy knew, would be rising within the hour. It was in its three-quarter phase and would provide enough light to illuminate the trail for a man who knew how it ran.

By the time the orange moon had pulled its face up above the distant eastern horizon, though, Sandy had been chafed raw by the unfamiliar ancient saddle, and the buckskin's swaying, shambling pace had been reduced to a heavy-footed slog. The animal could not carry on much longer, and Sandy could not either.

Almost with anger — at himself, the buckskin and especially Amos Coyne

— Sandy was forced to admit that he was going to have to make a dry night camp and let himself and the horse rest for at least a couple of hours.

The ground on the small clearing where Sandy swung down was hard, but no harder than the saddle he had been sitting. After stripping the horse of its gear, he let the weary animal scrounge for whatever scant graze it could find and rolled up in his single blanket with a tethering rope to the buckskin tied to his foot. He could not lose that horse, such as it was, and have a chance out in open country.

He did not sleep, but rested. The rocky ground, the chill of the night prevented any real chance of sleep. The buckskin slept, or so he thought. It was hard to tell — the animal seemed to have been half-asleep since they had begun this probably futile pursuit of Amos Coyne.

To Sandy it seemed that the plan was already doomed to failure. But what else could he have done? Coyne had left them high and dry in Durant, and he had probably killed Len Storch as well. Coyne would eventually pay for his dirty tricks if Sandy Rivers had anything to say about it. He reflected that Jerry Higgins and Turk at least had a roof over their heads tonight, thanks to Pete Faber's kindness and understanding, but they could not count on more than a single night's lodging. They would rise tomorrow in a strange town, hungry and broke. As for Sandy's own situation, well, it was not one to be envied . . .

His eyes flickered open. The shadow of a man passed in front of the distant moon. Sandy stiffened beneath his blanket and let his hand stretch toward his Colt revolver.

'Don't move,' a vaguely familiar voice said in a near growl, and the silhouette came nearer, boot heels sounding heavy against the rubble underfoot. 'There's no sense in moving. It seems you've found yourself a place to lie that's almost comfortable.'

Sandy's tension was eased only slightly by the man's manner, which did not seem angry or murderous. He sat up and stared at the newcomer's face. Finally, in the near-darkness, he made out a face he knew.

'Bobo?'

'It's me,' Bob Bodine, more commonly known among the Sky Box hands as Bobo, replied. 'Do you mind if I sit down?'

'If you can find a comfortable spot,' Sandy offered.

'I don't even care much about that. I'm to the point where I have to either sit down or fall down,' Bobo told him. And it seemed to be true. He sat with a sagging thump, shaking his head bitterly as he landed. There was blood on Bobo's face, Sandy noticed, showing as dark strings in the light of the moon.

'What are you doing out here, Bob?'

'Trying to make it to Durant,' the man answered. 'It seemed my only chance. You don't happen to have any water with you, do you?'

Sandy shifted and reached for one of his two canteens and handed it across to Bobo who drank greedily, then lowered the canteen with a guilty look on his face. 'Sorry, Sandy, I know you can't have a lot to spare. But I haven't had a drop of water in a day and a half.'

'Take another sip,' Sandy offered, and Bobo did so, corking the canteen when he was finished and handing it back.

'What happened to you, Bob?' Sandy asked.

'It was that crazy Amos Coyne, of course,' Bobo said, with unconcealed venom. 'Him and that bull whip of his. I asked him where you, Storch, Turk and Jerry were, and he told me you four had decided to leave us back in Durant. Which I knew wasn't so, because Turk, at least, wanted to head south again on his way back to Texas, and Jerry had hopes of hooking on permanently with the Sky Box.'

'So he whipped you?' Sandy asked in disbelief, although how he could doubt

Bobo's story after what had happened to Storch he could not have said. It was just that he had never run across a man with such blatant disregard of civilized behavior in all his years.

'Whipped me, grabbed my horse's reins, saying it was Sky Box stock, and turned me out onto the desert, saying that maybe it would teach me not to back-talk my bosses. The horse bolted — it's probably in no better shape than I am right now.'

'Was your horse Sky Box stock?'

'Sure it was. You remember that old Vincent Skye gathered us and told us to take any of his ponies we found useful. Said he wanted us riding the best horses we could on the cattle drive.'

'Yes, he did,' Sandy recalled. He had taken Skye up on the offer himself. The red roan he had been riding was gaunted out, and so he had taken the big gray horse from Skye's string as his primary mount for the cattle drive.

'Why did you even approach Coyne?' Sandy asked. 'I mean, we could have chosen to stay behind, stay drunk and chase skirts.'

'Because I know Amos Coyne,' Bobo said. 'I've ridden for Sky Box for a long time. Let me ask you this — who did Coyne kill?'

What a question! Did Bob Bodine know of trouble between Storch and the trail boss? Suspect something similar?

'I think he killed Len Storch,' Sandy told him. 'He had been whipped and then stabbed in the back. We figured it was Coyne's work. Why did you ask a question like that, Bob?'

'I never yet been on a trail drive with Coyne when somebody didn't fail to make it back,' Bobo said. His head had bowed to his drawn-up knees and he now sat motionless in the cool of night, a pathetic silhouette in the moonlight. When Bobo spoke again, his voice was muffled.

'What are you doing out here alone, Sandy?'

'Going after Amos Coyne.'

'Did I hear you right? What did he do

to you?' Bobo asked.

'Outside of taking our horses and leaving us on the side of the road to starve to death, you mean?'

Bobo nodded his head. 'All right. I see what you mean. It's the way Coyne does his job, Sandy. It's a damn shame, but in his mind, that's the way to go about it. He knows you three were hired on only for the trail drive, that the chances of you ever returning to Sky Box were small. He must have gotten a little careless this time. You probably weren't supposed to ever know what happened to your horses.'

'So he just returns our ponies to the home ranch?'

'Or sells them along the way — he's got the authority to do that. That puts a few hundred dollars extra in his pockets. He'll just say that you three pulled out and kept your horses.'

'What would old man Skye say to that?'

'It wouldn't be the first time he'd heard that. Besides, you did leave your own horses on the ranch for Sky Box use. Vince Skye would just cuss you a little, say he'd be more careful who he hired next year and drop it. He'd count the cash he made off this year's drive and be satisfied with that.'

'And Coyne keeps getting away with it?'

'Year after year,' Bobo said. 'He makes an extra four or five hundred a year with that trick alone, and a bonus from Skye for getting the herd through.'

'Still . . . ' Sandy Rivers was staring at the paling moon. 'Why would he go so far as to kill a man like Storch? That couldn't have profited Coyne any.'

'One more horse, one more bit of pay he could reclaim. Also Vince Skye is a decent man. He usually sends some money to the relatives of any man who happens to meet misfortune while working for the ranch. Of course, Coyne usually offers to deliver it to the bereaved. Vincent Skye is nearly eighty years old, you know; he doesn't often ride any more.'

'Coyne has it working for him in a dozen petty ways, doesn't he?'

'It adds up. I personally know that he has cut out a few calves over the years — he has enough unbranded mavericks that he could start his own ranch.'

'Then why stay with Sky Box?' Sandy wondered.

'Because there's still more money to be made in easier ways than working for it. As I said, Vince Skye is nearly eighty and he has only the one heir: his daughter Corrine. You must have seen her.'

'Not to notice.'

'Then you haven't seen her, because you'd remember Corrine Skye,' Bob Bodine told him. 'She is one beautiful little girl in a tight package, if you know what I mean.'

'Don't tell me — Coyne is cosying up to Corrine Skye,' Sandy said.

'He's trying his best. As far as I can tell, Corrine doesn't care a snap of her fingers for Coyne. But he probably has the old man's blessing and he'll keep trying.' There was a pause and then

Bobo said, 'Sandy?'

'Yeah?'

'To answer your original question, why did Coyne have to kill Len Storch, I can tell you why: Amos Coyne likes to kill. He enjoys being cruel to animals and people both. He loves to use that whip on whatever he can find. He's a cruel man and he takes his cruelty seriously.'

Sandy, who had seen Coyne needlessly whipping cattle along the trail and had witnessed the result of the flaying of Len Storch, done out of brutality if the man meant to kill Storch with a knife all along, listened to Bobo and could only slowly nod his head. He did not know any other such men, and he hoped never to run into one again.

Except one. Yes, he meant to meet up with Amos Coyne once again.

*   *   *

The moon was riding high when Sandy rose to his feet on cramped, chilled legs.

He figured the horse was rested enough to continue. And he had to continue if he hoped to make up ground on Amos Coyne. As Sandy hefted his blanket and saddle, Bob Bodine, who had been sleeping, opened an eye and looked at him.

'Planning on moving on, are you?' Bobo asked.

'I don't figure there's any time to lose,' Sandy answered, tossing his saddle onto the buckskin's back.

'Probably not.' Bob Bodine got to his feet like an arthritic old man. Coyne had obviously inflicted some serious damage on him. 'Will that horse carry double?'

Sandy swallowed the laugh that rose to his lips. 'I guess you haven't had a good look at it. He'll barely carry one, Bob. Why do you ask?'

'Because I want to go along. Sandy, I owe the man. Even if I can make it to Durant, I'd find myself in the same shape as Turk and Jerry Higgins, and that's the best I have to hope for. Going

51

with you, I'd have a chance to pay Coyne back.'

'It won't work, Bob. The horse can't carry double and that's that.'

'There's a chance I could find my own pony up ahead. It was startled and took off when my ruckus with Coyne began.'

'That doesn't seem like much of a chance, finding a horse out here, not even knowing which way it might have run.'

'I guess it isn't,' Bobo was forced to admit. 'The animal was well-trained, though, Sandy. I can usually whistle it up and he'll come.'

'Why didn't you try that before now?'

Bobo's expression was grave, slightly ashamed perhaps. 'Sandy, I just managed to escape with my life. I was hiding in the rocks and brush. I couldn't give my position away by whistling with armed men looking for me.'

'No,' Sandy said with understanding. 'You say 'men', Coyne wasn't alone in this, then?'

'No, he has three or four men who know how he works, and what he's trying to do — take over Sky Box — and they'll back him up whatever he does.'

Sandy was wearing a frown. 'I never noticed any of this funny business on the trail up to Durant.'

'Why would you? There was no point in him trying these maneuvers before he'd driven the herd to the trailhead.'

'But you keep riding for Sky Box!'

'I do. I ride for the brand. I was drifting in the wind before old Vince Skye took me on, gave me a place to sleep, to eat, and a feeling that I belonged somewhere . . . it was real important at that time, Sandy.'

'But you've never tried to talk to Skye about Coyne?'

'A word or two now and then, but Vince just laughed off my remarks. I told you, Amos Coyne is his pup and the presumed future husband of Corrine. It doesn't do a man much good to try to talk Coyne down to Vincent Skye.'

53

'I suppose not.' Sandy looked at the beaten, forlorn man standing alone in the desert darkness looking up at him without hope. It was against his better judgement, but he finally said, 'Clamber aboard, Bob. We'll try riding double for at least a little ways. Maybe you'll find your horse.' Sandy saw little chance of that, but what was a man to do? Of course, in the end they could wind up two men afoot in the wilderness, but the decision, rash as it was, had been made, and he steadied the horse as Bobo mounted heavily behind him.

The buckskin blew out sharply through its nostrils in annoyance, but once Sandy had started it forward, the beast labored on, moving at the same slow steady pace as before. At daybreak with the sun hanging low and red above the horizon, Bobo spoke up.

'We're getting close to where we were camped. You can make out the fresh hoofprints if you look. We can just follow them along, Sandy. Me, I'll be keeping an eye out for my pony.' Sandy only nodded his head. It seemed to him that Bobo's horse would probably have circled around, eventually falling in again with the other horses, but then he was no expert on how a horse's brain worked. They were like dogs and most other animals — they all had their own individual traits. Sandy had seen men shot dead and their horses standing over them, refusing to move. Others would run off, never to be seen again. He supposed it had something to do with how they were trained and how they'd been treated.

Sandy halted the buckskin every few miles to let the horse blow. He suggested that Bobo dismount when these pauses were made, but Bobo told him with sincerity, 'Sandy, I'm not sure I could get up again if I did. I'm hurting more than I was yesterday.'

Once when Sandy was sharing his canteen with Bobo after swinging down to give the horse a little relief, he took a good look at the Sky Box rider in the daylight. Bobo's face was bruised, his tan-colored shirt torn nearly to shreds by the lash of Amos Coyne's whip. His eyes appeared as dark, deeply sunken orbs in his gaunt face. The man needed rest and food if were to survive. With his mouth tight, Sandy hung the canteen back on the saddle horn and climbed aboard.

'Next time we stop, you're going to have to swing down and have something to eat.'

'I couldn't eat none of your food, Sandy. I seen how light you're traveling.'

'I've got twice what I need to travel on,' Sandy lied.

Later, as they rested and tried to make a meal of Sandy's poor stores, Sandy said, 'Maybe I should have just left you to go on to Durant on your own. You would have made it by now and found yourself some comfort.'

'You're regretting bringing me along?' Bobo asked from a seated position. His hat brim shadowed his unhappy face.

'I just mean that it's kind of crazy

— a man in the shape you are in trying to run Coyne down.'

After a few false starts, Bobo managed to get stiffly to his feet. There was a broken-toothed grin on his face. 'You know, Sandy, if I'm crazy to try to track the man down, what does that make you exactly?'

Sandy smiled, shrugged and rose himself. 'I don't know, Bob,' he said truthfully. 'Shall we travel on?'

'I've found a way to make it a little easier on all of us,' Bobo said. Sandy could now see that Bobo's eyes were fixed on some distant object unmoving against the lava-rock-strewn land. Bobo put two fingers to his lips and let out a shrill, penetrating whistle. The object in the distance stirred and, lifting its head, began to trot toward them.

'I told you he'd stand,' Bobo said proudly.

The horse, a neat little paint pony Sandy was familiar with, trotted right into their camp, tossing its head twice. Bobo staggered to the animal and put his arms around its neck. He looked to Sandy. 'Think we can spare a drop or two of water, Sandy? Little Cookie here has been dry since I left him.'

Sandy nodded and took the canteen back off the pommel. There wasn't much left in it, he noted. True he had a second canteen, but had planned on it being enough for one man and not two. They had crossed a creek on the drive up which was not many miles away, but it was a seasonal stream and hadn't been running that much water even then. Sky Box cattle and horses had turned the creek into a muddy wash in their passing. They would have to hope for the best.

Bobo had poured a few handfuls of water into his hat and was now holding it up for the horse to drink. Sandy decided to try again. 'You've got Cookie back now, Bob. Don't you think that you'd be better off riding to Durant?'

'And what would I do there, Sandy? I could sell my saddle for a few meals and a bed, I suppose. And when that money ran out, I'd maybe have to sell Cookie. Then one day I'd find myself busted and afoot. You know that town has no work to offer except when the herds are gathered, waiting for the train to roll in, and we both know no other ranch in the area has planned another trail drive for the rest of the year. You were in that position, same as Turk and Jerry Higgins. Do you really think that's a situation I want to find myself in?

'No,' Bobo said, shaking his head. 'You're stuck with me. I want Coyne every bit as bad as you do after what he did to me.'

Sandy only nodded. There was no arguing with the man. He did not wish to point out that Bobo would be lucky if he could stay in the saddle for another day. Things were just not getting any easier.

With both men mounted now, they turned away from their camp and headed westward once more, intent on following and destroying the maniac who had forced this hellish situation on them.

4

The land rose and fell, leveled off as they neared the summit pass, and the buckskin slogged on. Cookie didn't look to be in much better shape. The younger paint horse hadn't had enough feed and water the past few days. Bob Bodine looked worse than any of them. His head rolled and jerked as he clung to reins and pommel with both hands. He was a scarecrow riding, a starving, desperate avenging angel. At one point as they rode farther into brush country in the direction of the little creek, Bobo spoke up.

'You were right, Sandy. I shouldn't have come. I'm never going to make it to Sky Box and I'll be of no help if you get into it with Amos Coyne and his men.'

Sandy looked away for a few moments, then pasted on an unconvincing smile. 'You'll feel better after we have some water. You're healing all the time, remember. Your strength is bound to come back.'

Well, they said there were white lies. What else could he have said to the beaten man riding beside him? If they did manage to find good water in the creek, the best plan would be for Bobo to camp there for a day or two, try to get well. Sandy himself was set on continuing on as rapidly as he could, and that meant staying in the saddle for as many hours as the buckskin could carry him.

In mid-afternoon, they dipped down into a wash toward the creek which had no name that Sandy knew of. Its aspect was not promising. There was no sign of the sun glinting on water, nor could he smell it. There was some scent there, however; the lethargic buckskin lifted its head and stumbled on at a slightly quickened pace. They found what Sandy had expected — the remains of a creek, red mud and no sign of flowing water.

When Sandy dismounted, the buckskin began pawing at the mud. Sandy got to hands and knees and helped it to dig. After a while a puddle of muddy water appeared and then widened. Sandy wouldn't have drunk from it, but the buckskin did not mind. It lowered its muzzle and tested what they had found. Sandy turned to the spiritless man sitting the paint pony's saddle.

'Bob? There might be enough water here to do our horses some good.'

'All right,' Bobo said, lifting a listless hand. 'I'll lead Cookie over there.' Still Bobo lingered in the saddle, not moving, and it took Sandy a few seconds to realize that it was because he could not move — or was afraid to try getting down from the saddle. He walked to the paint pony and offered Bobo a hand.

'Let's do this while we can, Bob. There's no water to be found for at least another twenty miles.'

'All right. You're right,' Bob mumbled, but he still did not move. Cookie had lifted his head as well and now tossed his mane emphatically. If the buckskin was drinking, it wanted to drink too. Sandy patted Bobo's knee.

'Come on, old soldier, get down. We'll rest here for a while.'

Bobo nodded again and let the reins slip from his fingers. Sandy nearly had to catch him as Bobo tried to swing down. He led the staggering man toward the shade of a clump of thickly growing manzanita and sat him there while he returned to try to open up the waterhole more. Digging with his hands between the muzzles of the two horses, Sandy was rewarded with a wider, deeper puddle of a pond where clearer water stood. It was enough for the ponies, at least.

Rising he walked back to where Bobo lay on his back, hat over his face. Sandy wiped his muddy hands on the stubble grass that grew there and on his jeans before sitting down beside his motionless companion. Sandy's face was trickling sweat in the dry heat of the day. The little bit of extra exertion had been enough to start the perspiration trickling down his chest and under his arms. His shirt now cooled with the light gust of a breeze that had risen. He swatted away a menacing wasp and settled back on his elbows, watching Bobo closely.

He thought that the man had nearly played out his string. His breathing caused his lips to flutter. The sound was somewhere between a heavy snore and a death-rattle. What was there to do with him? He could not leave him alone out in this wild country, but he knew that Bobo would only slow him down in his pursuit of Amos Coyne.

Sandy was going to have to make a choice: leave his friend to die, or run down Amos Coyne and kill him. It wasn't much of a choice. A blue and gold dragonfly sped past him following the course of the creek. Sandy watched it until it rounded a curve in the creek, then returned his gaze to Bob Bodine. The branches of the manzanita shrubs cast shifting shadows across Bobo's supine body. Bobo's face still carried scabbed reminders of the brutality Amos Coyne had inflicted on him.

Without removing the hat from over his eyes, Bobo spoke, saying, 'Go after him, Sandy. You were right. I'm not up to this ride.'

'You'll be all right, after you rest for a little while.'

'Take Cookie and go, Sandy. Leave the buckskin horse behind. Him and me — we've both had it.'

'Bob . . . '

'I mean it,' Bobo snapped. 'Get after Coyne! Me and the buckskin, we'll stay behind, Maybe in a couple of days we'll both be rested enough to travel on.'

It was no time to argue. Both men knew the truth of their situation. 'I'll leave you a canteen,' Sandy said. 'I'll fill it at the seep hole.'

'Do that. Maybe a handful of food if you think you can spare it. But get the man, Sandy. Do that for me.' Sandy nodded and rose, feeling ill-rested himself. Reluctantly, but with deadly purpose he started away from the injured man. 'Take good care of Cookie,' were the last words Sandy heard Bobo say.

Sandy stripped the buckskin of its gear and tethered the horse near to Bobo, with enough length of rope lead to allow it to reach the waterhole. The buckskin was indifferent to all of it. Sandy did not bother to switch saddles. Cookie sported a regular Western saddle, a welcome relief from the broken McClellan Sandy had been sitting for nearly two days.

And the younger horse was ready and eager to run. Sandy guided it across the muddy creek bottom and up the far side of the gully and then, with one last glance back at Bobo, he rode out onto flat open land.

Sandy felt a little guilty about the entire episode, but he was grateful to fate which had delivered a smooth-riding, quick young pony to him. They covered ground quickly now across mostly level land, Cookie showing no aversion to having a strange rider on its back, a new pair of hands on its reins. It was nearing sundown, the shadows long on the plains when Sandy spotted something familiar to him.

The small pueblo he thought was called La Paloma stood alone on the wide land, a collection of squat humble adobes they had passed on the drive east. They had stayed clear of it so the villagers would not be annoyed by the huge herd of cattle and the dust it kicked up, and also because in a town of any size there are temptations for cowboys who have been long on the trail. Sandy felt obligated to ride on through the night, but it was obvious that Cookie had been slowing down, and he could not run the eager young pony into the ground. Sandy decided to spend a few hours, possibly the entire night in La Paloma, using his last few dollars to see that Cookie was well fed and well rested.

For himself he could use a meal if one could be found at a reasonable price. After the dry food he'd been chewing along the trail, almost anything would be welcome, and the Mexicans were noted for their cooking. Sandy slowed the horse as he approached the little town, watched as kids and their dogs scampered for home and men in wide sombreros sauntered on their own way, probably summoned by the same urgings as Sandy's for a home-cooked supper and a little rest after their day's work.

He briefly envied the men their settled way of life, then began looking for a stable and a place to sleep that accommodated strangers in the pueblo. He halted Cookie at the head of what he took to be the main street: a dusty, rutted road crowded by two rows of about six buildings facing each other. With Cookie quivering slightly beneath him, Sandy listened for certain sounds — music, laughter — and tried to detect beckoning scents. He thought that he had identified a cantina and a restaurant — probably one and the same by all indications, and used his knees to start Cookie on again, letting the horse now use its own senses to guide them.

Cookie would be able to scent or hear other horses and smell fresh hay and identify a stable or corral, whichever the town had to offer travelers, and he let the paint pony choose its own path through toward a pole and plaster stable which housed six other horses. None of them wore the Sky Box brand.

After stabling Cookie, Sandy started out along the streets of La Paloma. The sun behind him was fading. A deep reddish glow hung over the town, reflecting off the white adobe buildings. Somewhere a rooster said goodnight to the day and another cock answered it as if responding to a challenge. A small brown dog not much larger than a cat scooted away at Sandy's approach, yipping across its shoulder as it scurried away into the purple shadows of the alley. Distantly a guitar was playing a soft, sad Spanish tune.

It seemed a restful, peaceful night.

People gathered together and talked of the small events of their days. Sandy Rivers was not so comfortable. In any strange town a traveling man will feel a little uneasy not knowing the situation around him, or which people could be considered trustworthy.

It was not running into unknown enemies that weighed on Sandy as he strode the main street of La Paloma, however; it was the possibility of stumbling across men that he did know too well. He did not expect to encounter Amos Coyne in La Paloma, though it was possible. There was a good chance that a few stragglers from the trail herd might have decided to take some time out of the saddle in the pueblo, not an infrequent occurrence for men who had spent months at hard labor and were due to return to the routine of ranch life. While they had a few dollars and the opportunity, they would be willing to pass idle time in a place like La Paloma before returning to a working cowboy's drudgery.

Sandy entered a small warm restaurant which he had identified from the spicy scents in the air. The place had only four round tables and a long banquet-style setting along one wall. The dark-faced waitress wore a black dress and white apron and a harried scowl. Sandy could see why. She was trying to set the tables and sweep up at once. The restaurant was not open for business yet. In La Paloma, as in most warmer climes, the people did not eat their evening meal until the sun was well down and the air cooler.

However, the waitress exchanged her scowl for a smile and seated Sandy at a corner table, away from the heat emanating from the open kitchen. She offered no menu — if the place had such an item — and briefly explained that the cook had just started. Sandy was not a particular diner on this night. He shrugged away all of her apologies.

In the end he was served with the best they could offer just then, warmed flour tortillas and a bowl of pinto beans along with a mug of almost-cool beer. It tasted fine to a man who had gone long without a prepared meal of any kind. And it was a very inexpensive meal. All in all just what Sandy had hoped for.

Back out on the street, Sandy looked up and down the dark row of buildings. The man at the stable and the waitress had both told him that there was a small inn in La Paloma where he could find a bed for the night, but their English had not been good, nor had Sandy's kitchen Spanish been up to the task of making directions clear.

The street was quiet, the air cooling nicely. From a cantina another guitar — or the same one — sounded, accompanied by someone shaking a pair of maracas. Sandy didn't care much for Mexican music, but on this night it was enjoyable to hear, especially after the long silent nights on the desert.

A buggy drawn by a high-stepping white horse passed, apparently carrying a pair of high-born Spaniards. The man wore a dark suit and glaringly white, ruffled shirt, the woman a dress of muted blue and a lacy black mantilla over her head and shoulders. A small kid with a wooden box appeared, asking if Sandy needed his boots shined. He did, but the shine wouldn't last long and he hadn't the change to spare.

All in all there was a pleasant, subdued aspect about La Paloma, Sandy thought. He made his way farther to where he believed the hotel might be found, and by deciphering the sign painted on the white face of a two-story adobe building, deduced that he had found it.

The rooms to let sat above a cantina — the source of the music. He could hear men shouting in appreciation of the guitarist as he passed through the saloon toward the hotel desk beyond. The room smelled of tobacco and beer. Neither was that an unpleasant scent to Sandy, although he did not use tobacco. It seemed a necessary part of the conviviality somehow.

Passing through an archway he discovered the hotel desk. A man dressed in the style of a cowboy was leaning against it, his elbows on its edge, his eyes fixed on Sandy. Sandy's mouth tightened. He knew the man at once.

Randall Chandler had ridden with them on the trail east. Chandler wore a long unkempt red mustache, and a holstered Colt rode low on his hip. He was wearing a pair of sun-faded black jeans and a blue-checked shirt. He was no friend of Sandy's.

Chandler was a close ally of Amos Coyne, or at least they gave that impression. Bobo had told Sandy that Coyne had three or four men riding with him who were loyal enough to Coyne, or greedy enough to assist him in his schemes. Chandler would have been among Sandy's first guesses as to who they were.

'Took your time getting here,' was Randall Chandler's greeting.

'What do you mean, Chandler?'

'I saw you ride in to town something over an hour ago. I recognized the pony. Stolen, isn't it?'

'No, it's not stolen,' Sandy said, growing heated. Chandler had removed his elbows from the counter and stood up straight, studying him. 'It's a Sky Box horse, isn't it?' Sandy said. 'I work for Sky Box.'

'No you don't. I happen to know that you were fired off the crew back in Durant.' Chandler turned his head and made a gesture as if he were spitting, but his mouth was dry. Sandy had never thought of Chandler as menacing, in fact he had given little thought to the ranch hand, but there was something about him now that made Sandy wary. He let his hand inch closer to his own pistol. Chandler noticed this and something that might have been a smile twitched at the corner of his mouth.

'Where'd you get that horse, Rivers?' Chandler wanted to know.

Not wanting to go into the whole

story, Sandy shrugged and said, 'Found it loose on the desert. It beat what I was riding and so I switched to the paint. It didn't matter whose horse it was — I was riding back to Sky Box anyway.'

'Come on,' Chandler said belligerently. 'You know whose horse that was.'

'Sure I do,' Sandy admitted. 'It was Bob Bodine's pony.'

'So, what did you do with Bobo?' Chandler asked. He was easing nearer to Sandy, something the younger man did not care for.

'I didn't do anything to him,' Sandy protested. He had an idea now of where this conversation was heading.

'No?' Chandler said, standing close enough now to Sandy that he could smell the dried sweat and tobacco residue on him. Chandler made that spitting gesture again and then turned his cold dark eyes on Sandy once more. 'I think you killed Bobo and took his horse.'

'Why would I — ?'

'You were broke and down on your

luck and here comes Bobo riding a spry young paint pony — just what you needed — and so you took the opportunity and killed the man.'

'I did nothing of the sort.'

'So you only stole his horse? Is that right? Stole a Sky Box pony. They still hang men for that offense, Rivers. A man alone on foot doesn't stand a chance in wild country. It's the same as murder. One way or another you killed Bobo.'

'Did I? No, but you might talk to Amos Coyne about who might have killed Bob. Though I expect you already know all about it. You were there when it happened, weren't you?'

Outside of a flicker of his eyelids, Chandler did not react to that. 'What are you talking about, Rivers?'

'Bob Bodine wasn't dead when I came across him. He told me what Coyne did.'

'Bobo must have been out of his head . . . or maybe it's you who is,' Chandler said. Then he shrugged slightly and repositioned his hat on his head, thumbing it back. 'Maybe we won't hang you just now, not in a strange town. But you'd be well-advised to stay wide of Sky Box, Rivers. Over there you'll surely hang for killing Bobo and stealing his horse.'

With the threat delivered, Chandler turned back toward the cantina, sauntering away toward where the music played and the beer and tequila flowed. Well, Sandy thought, I've been warned. Putting it out of his mind as well as he could, he dug his hand into his pocket where the last of his coins rested. There was so little that he doubted he could even take a bed in the hotel. In the morning he had to see that the stable was paid for taking care of Cookie. Thinking of the horse led him to believe that he could not let it out of his sight for the night. He had it in mind to return to the stable and bargain with the man there for a place to sleep in the hayloft.

From out of a back room, a short,

very thin Mexican man peered out and then slipped through the door to return to his place behind the counter. Apparently he had not liked the look of Randall Chandler either and had decided to absent himself from the area. The little man asked, 'May I help you please, *señor*?'

'No,' Sandy answered, 'I've changed my mind.'

So it was that Sandy Rivers, after striking a deal with the stablehand, spent the night in the loft, watching over Cookie, a nervous restlessness keeping him from getting much sleep. Once, near dawn, the hinges of the stable door squeaked a complaint and Sandy saw the narrow figure of a man peering into the darkness of the building. Then, after a moment's look, he left again, closing the door.

Sandy thought he recognized the man: Jordy Cavett, a Sky Box rider who was also close to Amos Coyne, but in that light he could not be sure. If so, there were at least two Sky Box men in

La Paloma. They must have their horses picketed out somewhere, perhaps behind the hotel. No matter, Sandy had at least two men to concern himself with. All the more reason to hit the trail early and put some distance between himself and these possible adversaries.

Sunrise was still only a vague orange glow in the single high window of the stable when Sandy led Cookie from his stall and spread the saddle blanket over his back. The stablehand had appeared from somewhere and he watched with sleepy eyes as Sandy completed his work. They haggled briefly over the money due, but as it became evident to the stableman that the change in Sandy's palm was all that he possessed and he remembered the bribe he had taken to allow Sandy to bed down in the loft the night before, he finally gave in, shrugged and took the coins as his due.

Sandy swung aboard the paint pony and walked the animal out into the dim glow of dawn's light. He turned

Cookie's head away from the main street of La Paloma and rode westward out onto the empty dry grasslands toward the far distant Sky Box Ranch.

He did not know what lay ahead of him. He could not predict the outcome of his arrival on the home ranch. All he knew was that Turk, Jerry Higgins, Bob Bodine and the ghost of Len Storch expected it of him.

The land was raw, harsh and empty. As was Sandy Rivers's heart.

5

The earlier passing of the Sky Box herd had provided a well-defined empty swath of trail across the plateau. A blind man could have followed it, but it did little to comfort Sandy to have his way so well defined. It was like a road to hell, following the flattened earth, sheared dry grass, the waterholes trampled to mud, to a place where accusations, humiliation and possibly death by gun or rope awaited him. It would have been easy to turn off the trail to Sky Box and simply ride away to nowhere at all. Except . . .

There were a lot of men depending on him to speak for them and try to correct injustice. Those he had left back in Durant, those he had left along the trail. And Sandy felt an obligation to the Sky Box owner, old Vincent Skye who always treated his men fairly, and who was apparently now in the grip of a conniving, deceitful man he trusted. Oddly, Sandy found himself thinking also of the ranch-owner's daughter, Corrine Skye, whom he did not remember ever having seen. She would not have mingled with the ordinary trail drivers.

But she must have been trusting to her father's business to provide for her. It seemed, from what Sandy had been told, that she did not like Amos Coyne much, but that her father favored him as a match for her. Sandy had pity for any woman condemned to spend her life with the cruel Amos Coyne. Would he treat his wife as he treated animals and men? It seemed likely.

How was he — Sandy — to deliver all of his observations to Vincent Skye and his daughter? Would they laugh at him? Drive him off the ranch afoot? Or worse — for by now Amos Coyne had certainly returned to the Sky Box, earning the owner's thanks for a job well done. Coyne's version of what had happened along the trail would be the first to be delivered and the most likely to be believed. Sandy had no allies on the ranch, no one to stand up for him. He barely knew most of the regular ranch hands. Certainly there was none who would vouch for Sandy's character.

Still he rode on, the sun riding high in a pale-blue sky, the paint pony moving easily beneath him as they continued in a straight line toward Sky Box. Right into the realm of Amos Coyne.

And Coyne was definitely a maniac, a killer and a cruel master. He was also, by all accounts, shrewd and calculating, which made him doubly dangerous. Sandy doubted that his wild tales of Coyne lashing men, stealing their horses for sale, rustling Sky Box cattle would carry much weight with Vincent Skye. But it had to be done. It had to be tried!

It was at twilight time that he first saw Sky Box again after being away for nearly a week. Cookie seemed to know where he was, for he headed directly toward the horse barn which rested a hundred yards or so from Skye's big white house sheltered by oak trees. In the purple of dusk the house seemed to have an unhealthy pallor. The big oak trees were black silhouettes against a pagan sky. Sandy tried to shake these thoughts away, knowing he was letting his mood influence his observations.

Reaching the red barn he halted Cookie and swung wearily down from the saddle. There was no one inside. Sky Box had no need to guard the stables. No one would dare to come upon this land for the sake of a few horses — not with twenty or thirty armed cattlemen around.

After stabling Cookie and forking some new hay into the paint's bin, he looked around hopefully for his own gray horse, but the animal had not been returned to the barn. Looking farther along the aisle, Sandy found his red roan, the only horse he actually owned, the one he had ridden in on, looking for work on the Sky Box drive. The animal looked filled out, sleek and bright-eyed now, quite a bit different. The red roan seemed to remember Sandy well enough, for it dropped its muzzle to nudge Sandy's shoulder. Sandy stroked its neck and promised it better treatment in the future.

Behind him the barn door opened wide once again to allow a man carrying a lantern high to enter. Sandy knew him. The young-old man was named Nathan Arbuckle. Young-old because Nate moved with a shuffling pace and could not hold himself erect. At one time he had taken a bad spill from a roping horse and damaged his hip and spine in a way that could never be repaired. Nate had a long face, a long nose. As usual he was whiskered. Nate had only a nodding acquaintance with his razor.

'Howdy, Nate!' Sandy said in greeting, and Nate lifted his eyes, surprised to see him. At one time Sandy had helped Nate, who was now the yard man on Sky Box, unload a stack of heavy planks from a delivery wagon. He was the nearest thing to a friend Sandy had on the ranch. Now he smiled with recognition.

'I'll be damned,' Arbuckle said with a grin. 'Never thought to see you again, Sandy. Come back looking for steady work?'

'Not really,' Sandy said without explaining further. The two shook hands. 'I need to ask you something, Nate.'

'Ask away,' Nate said cheerfully. He seated himself clumsily on a bale of hay, placing his lantern beside him.

'I need to see Vincent Skye. How would I go about that?'

Nate grinned and shook his head. 'Walk up to the front door, knock and ask,' he suggested.

'Suppose I couldn't? Tell me, Nate, is Amos Coyne back yet?'

'I can't say. I haven't seen him, but that don't mean anything. Why do you ask?'

'I just don't want to run into him.'

'I'd be just as happy if I never saw him again the rest of my life,' Nate said, his voice growing bitter.

'You know that much about him, do you?'

'I've been on Sky Box five years now,' Nate answered with a nod. 'I've heard all the stories.'

'I wish I'd heard some of them before I hired on for the trail drive,' Sandy said.

'What would you have done different, Sandy? Forked that old roan you were riding and keep wandering across the desert? Your roan looks good now, don't he? I've been giving it a little extra care.'

'You have? I thank you for that.'

'Well,' Nate said honestly, 'I was thinking he might fall to me.'

'What do you mean?' Sandy asked with a frown.

'You were on a drive with Coyne, weren't you? Who knew if you'd be coming back?'

'Yes, well, that's what I need to talk to Vincent Skye about — the way Coyne treats his men.'

Nate wagged his head heavily. His eyes lifted again. 'It wouldn't do you any good, Sandy. Old man Skye won't hear a word against the man.'

'I've got to try, Nate. I know he killed one man along the way and possibly another on the ride back.'

'See it happen, did you?' Nate Arbuckle asked.

'No, but the one I helped to bury had whiplash marks all over his body. The other man — Bob Bodine — was riding with me until he just couldn't do it any more. He told me that it was Coyne who whipped him to within an inch of his life.'

'Old Bobo!' Nate was startled. 'He was a regular ranch hand, not a trail drover.'

As if that made a difference. Drovers, it seemed, were considered expendable. Nate asked, 'Did Bobo tell you why Coyne did it?'

'Does Coyne need a reason?' Sandy asked, and Nate wagged his head in response.

'What you was asking about, though,' Nate said, 'are you thinking of finding a way to get to Vince Skye without somebody seeing you?'

'That was my idea.'

Nate continued to shake his head as if he were conversing with a crazy man. Perhaps he was. 'The old man ain't well. Mostly he stays in bed these days.'

'I know that. He hasn't been well for a long time.'

'No, but he's a lot worse now, Sandy, from what the house help tells me.'

'I'm sorry about that, and I don't mean to upset Skye, but I think he has the right to know what goes on when Coyne is trail master.'

'You're right, I suppose,' Nate said without enthusiasm. His eyes met Sandy's determined gaze. 'OK, here's a way you can try to go about it if you really feel you have to.'

'I have to.'

'Have you ever been inside that house, Sandy?' Sandy Rivers shook his head negatively. 'All right — here's how it's set up. The front part of the house has their living room, Vince Skye's office, a small library and such for family use. The back part of the house is mostly taken up by the kitchen, larder and a laundry room. There is a staircase that reaches the upstairs bedrooms from either side. It is in the shape of an 'A'. Meals can be brought up that way, linen and such as is called for from the kitchen and laundry without disturbing Skye and any guests he might have.'

'I see,' Sandy said thoughtfully. 'You're saying that if I can get through the back door and slip through the kitchen, I can reach Skye's bedroom that way and not be seen by Corrine or Coyne or anyone else who might be around.'

'That's what I'm saying, but there's no certainty you can get through the kitchen. The cook keeps a cleaver, Sandy.'

'I'll chance it,' Sandy replied with a faint smile. 'Won't the cook be about finished for the day?'

Glancing at the open door where the skies showed only a faint thin band of purple color above the western mountains, Nate Arbuckle said, 'He should be, I'd think. If they dined late, lingering over their meals, the housemaid might still be hovering to remove the dishes from the table.'

Sandy thought about it. If Vincent Skye were confined to his room, there wouldn't be much lingering at the table. Unless there were company visiting — and Sandy had seen no carriages or strange horses around — Corrine Skye would have eaten by herself, and the meal would not have been formally served.

'I'll wait an hour or so, and then I'll give it a try,' Sandy said.

'There's six rooms altogether upstairs. Skye's bedroom is the third back on the left side as you get to the landing.'

'Thanks, Nate. You've been a help.'

'I feel like I'm helping a man who's

intent on setting off a powder keg,'
Nate said.

* * *

Nate was up and moving about, still
tending to the horses, each of which he
stopped to talk to and give a stroke
when Sandy judged enough time had
passed to make his try. The ranch was
quiet as he stepped out into the night.
Inside the distant bunkhouse, a few of
the boys were cutting up, probably
playing loudly at cards, but the sounds
were greatly muted by distance, and the
house itself sat still in the darkness, as
silent as if it were deserted. Crossing
the dry grass at the back of the house,
Sandy glanced up and saw that there
was a lantern burning in the window
of the third room back. Good; on top of
everything else, he did not wish to have
to awaken Vincent Skye to deliver his
bad news.

Would Skye call for help and have
Sandy escorted from the house before

he had a chance to even speak his piece? There was no telling. Sandy did not really know the ranch owner. There was no knowing what sort of ill-temper his illness might have left him with.

Easing toward the back of the house, Sandy listened for movement behind the black windows. There was no reason for anyone to be up and moving around in the unlighted kitchen, or at least he thought not, but you never knew. The silence held. The only yard dog, a mixed-breed hound named Duke, had been mauled by a black bear and not yet replaced. No alarm was raised as he stepped up onto the rear steps leading to the kitchen.

The door was unlocked, and it swung open easily on oiled hinges. Heart pounding, Sandy slipped into the warmth of the house. The kitchen smelled strongly of lye soap and, more faintly, of roast beef, both of which Sandy reflected he was in need of. He waited a full minute, hoping his eyes would adjust to the darkness. There was a sliver of lantern light from beyond showing beneath an inner door, but it did nothing to illuminate the darkness of the back of the house. He eased his way along the hallway, able to see only a few sharp corners and indistinguishable forms. Starlight tried to spray some feeble light into the room, but was balked by the blinds pulled tight over the windows.

Moving more by touch than vision he kept his hands stretched out in front of him and was eventually rewarded by the touch of polished wood beneath his fingers at the right height and in the proper location for a banister. Glancing up, he could again make out a narrow, faint ribbon of yellow light beneath a closed door. His eyes, slightly more accustomed to the darkness now, showed him a flight of stairs leading upward and he crept up them, taking only one step at a time, trying to keep his boots silent against the wood.

Reaching the closed door which should conceal a landing, he paused, gripped the iron door handle and cautiously twisted it. Without a sound the door opened and Sandy found himself standing in a dimly lighted, carpeted hallway. Another set of stairs, these carpeted as well, led down to the main part of the house. Sandy's breath was coming tightly. From somewhere he thought he heard the murmuring of voices, but if they were coming from below or beyond he could not tell. In the near-silence, with his emotions as tightly wound as they were, he thought he could just be imagining them.

Out in open country he had no fear of rushing into a dangerous situation, no trepidation about trying to cross dangerous ground, but inside the house he felt completely out of his element. He would never have made a burglar. Those men must have a peculiar sort of foolish nerve.

Not knowing which door along the hall might hide a man with a gun, he moved swiftly toward the third door to his left. There was no point in inching his way along. Striding toward the door, he saw a thin sketch of light beneath. He hesitated. Someone was awake, alerted? That someone might be holding a pistol, just waiting for Sandy to open the door. He did not want to rap on it and alert others who might be in the house — Coyne? Taking a deep breath he twisted the brass knob and entered the bedroom of Vincent Skye.

'That's far enough,' he was warned, before he had taken two steps into the room. The warning was emphasized by the sharper command of a Colt revolver being cocked. 'Make another move and I'll blow you away.'

Involuntarily, Sandy's hands lifted to the height of his shoulders. In front of him, lying on his bed was an older, grayer Vincent Skye, his blue eyes cloudy, curious. The old man was covered only by a white sheet. He looked sepulchral beneath it, his body shrunken. His white hands with enlarged knuckles lay on the sheet, blue-veined and partially curved arthritically inward. He held no weapon;

his eyes held no promise or warning, but only vacant interest in Sandy's arrival.

The person sitting to one side, the one who had issued the warning, had a pistol all right. A steel-blue Colt .44, its muzzle unwaveringly trained on Sandy Rivers.

It was Sandy's first meeting with Corrine Skye.

He turned his head slightly to look at her, careful to keep his hands high. No one had been exaggerating when she was described as beautiful. Dark-haired, slender, with high cheekbones, full lower lip and clear blue eyes, she wore on this night a dark-green, black-trimmed skirt and jacket with the kind of do-ups that Sandy had heard described as 'frogs'.

Just now those blue eyes were flashing with a light, not reflected from the lantern on the far table but gleaming with some inner source. Her mouth was tight. The Colt in her fine, long-fingered hand had not wavered.

'Who are you and what do you want

here?' Corrine demanded.

'My name's Sandy Rivers, and I was hired on to work the trail drive to Durant. I just got back.'

'You look it,' Corrine said, causing Sandy to reflect on his personal appearance for the first time in quite a while.

'I remember you,' Vincent Skye said, his voice sounding like a scraping bow on a cello's strings.

'All right,' Corrine said, her words still sharp. 'Now we know who you are, but what are you doing here — in my father's room in the night?'

'I felt I had to talk to your father about some . . . things that happened along the trail and at its end.'

'Things! Like what?' Corrine demanded. 'Didn't you get enough beans to eat?'

Sandy's caution fell away. He said angrily, 'Things like men being bullwhipped and murdered,' he said forcefully. 'Friends of mine.'

'Can't you see that my father is exhausted?' Corrine said, rising from the corner chair. 'The last thing he needs is some saddle tramp disturbing his rest with some wild tales.' Her eyes reflected protectiveness. Sandy had lowered his hands now. He started to answer her harshly, but from the bed Vincent Skye's voice sounded again.

'Let the boy have his say, Corrine.'

'All right,' Corrine said with unhappy resignation, sitting again, the heavy pistol she held still in shooting position.

'First,' Vincent Skye asked, holding up a pale hand, 'did you ride back with Amos Coyne?'

'No, sir, I haven't seen him.'

'He's probably taken a few days to rest up in Durant,' Corrine suggested.

'No,' Sandy said firmly. 'He's not in Durant, just a couple of men he abandoned there.'

'Why isn't he back, then?' Corrine asked. Now a slight line of worry was etched across her fine brow.

'I couldn't say,' Sandy answered. 'It would only be speculation on my part.'

'Speculation as to what?' Corrine demanded. Vincent Skye's hand twitched, calling for silence. The old man spoke again, his eyes more alert now.

'You said something about men being bull-whipped and one killed.'

'Yes, sir. Bob Bodine was whipped to within an inch of his life. He told me that Coyne was responsible.'

'Bobo . . . is he back, too?' Corrine wanted to know.

'No. He couldn't make it back.'

'Bobo is a good hand,' Vincent Skye muttered.

'The other man I'm speaking of, Len Storch, got himself whipped half to death, but it seems Coyne got tired of wielding the lash and just finished him off with a knife in the back.'

Vincent Skye grimaced and closed his eyes. Corrine again rose to her feet. 'Look how you're disturbing my father, bursting in here with these wild accusations. I take it you have some sort of grudge against Amos Coyne, but why bring these wild stories here now? Have you even an iota of proof as to what you're saying?'

Sandy reached into the pocket of his leather vest and withdrew an item he had been carrying since Durant. He displayed the bone-handled knife he had pulled from Len Storch's back. There were still bloodstains on the ivory-white hilt.

'Have you ever seen this before?' Sandy asked.

6

The blade of the knife gleamed dully in the light cast by the corner lantern. Vincent Skye stretched out a pale, unsteady hand.

'Will you let me see that?' the old man asked. Sandy stepped nearer to hand it to Skye, saw the man's face draw down with concern, watched his eyes close.

'Father?' Corrine said with concern.

'I gave this knife to Amos on Christmas a year ago,' Skye said without opening his eyes.

'That means nothing,' Corrine said, trying for a bit of encouragement. 'We don't know where this man got the knife.'

'I pulled it out of Len Storch's bloody, dead body.'

'So you say,' Corrine said, glancing at her father whose eyes, now open, showed concern. 'Do you have any witnesses to back up that story?' she demanded.

'Yes, I do. At least five. The bartender at the saloon, for example — '

'Who, of course, can't be here,' Corrine scoffed. Sandy went on as if she had not spoken.

'There's a well-known citizen of Durant, a gambler named Jake Koons.' Corrine simply smirked, knowing Koons would not be here either. The doubt in her eyes was growing into an angry expression. Sandy turned his eyes to Vincent Skye, hoping to convince him.

'Sitting with me at the table were two Sky Box drovers — Turk Bemis and Jerry Higgins by name. Turk helped me bury Storch.'

A harsh smile had returned to Corrine's lips. 'Neither can they be here to substantiate this story of yours,' she sneered.

'No,' Sandy said soberly. 'They can't be here because Amos Coyne spirited away their mounts as well as mine, leaving us stranded in Durant.'

'Why would he do that?' Corrine asked, her interest a mask for mockery.

'Because he didn't want us returning here, and, Bob Bodine told me, it's his usual practice to take Sky Box horses at the end of trail and return home to say that the drovers have simply ridden off with them.'

'Why would he do that?' Corrine asked. Her faith in Coyne seemed to have eroded slightly. Perhaps she remembered other drives when Coyne had made such reports.

'For a few hundred dollars or extra stock for his ranch.'

'He has no ranch,' Corrine Skye said coldly, as if her point was proven.

'He plans on having one,' Sandy told her. 'Bob Bodine says Coyne has been herding unbranded calves off the Sky Box for a long time. That plan is, of course, his secondary one to be used if he cannot marry you, Corrine, and take over the Sky Box after — '

'After I'm in the ground,' Vincent Skye finished, saving Sandy the embarrassment of saying it. 'Our spring gather has been down a lot the last three years,

I've noticed. I wonder — '

'Oh, Father, you can't believe Amos would engage in these shabby machinations,' said Corrine. Sandy had to wonder why she was protecting Amos Coyne so strongly if, as Bob Bodine had told him, she had no interest at all in the man as a future husband.

There was a silence after that during which Vincent Skye was quite thoughtful. His body was failing him, but his mind was alert enough. He directed a question at Sandy.

'Didn't you say that you were sure that Amos wasn't staying over in Durant for a little rest after the drive?'

'No, sir. He and his crew were gone the morning after the stock train pulled out.'

'Then where is he?' Vincent Skye asked of no one in particular. 'And where are the proceeds from this year's cattle sale?'

Looking flustered, Corrine Skye rose, placed the gun aside and hoisted her skirts to sweep out of the room, silently angry. It was not clear who or what she was angry with. Sandy watched her go. Skye kept his eyes on the door long after his daughter had gone out and closed it behind her.

'Rivers?'

'Yes, sir?'

'You're sure of everything you have been saying?'

'Most of it. It was Bob Bodine who told me the rest.'

'Will Bobo be coming back?'

Sandy shook his head worriedly. 'I don't know. I hope so. I had to leave him out in the wild country with a broken-down horse. He had been savagely whipped. Apparently he criticized something that Coyne had done. Coyne didn't want to take the chance of him relating it to you. If Amos Coyne didn't love using that bullwhip so much he would have simply shot Bob and be done with it. The problem was that Bob was tough enough to make his escape afterwards. That's when we met. His body was . . . badly injured,' Sandy said, remembering the gruesome marks the lashing had left across Bob Bodine's flesh.

'I'd like to have talked to Bobo,' Skye said.

'He told me that he'd tried to hint at some of these problems with Coyne before, but you would hear nothing against Coyne.'

'Did he?' Skye lifted a hand and rubbed his bloodless brow. 'My fault. I was busy, always too busy, it seems. A man rushes through life trying to get as much done as he possibly can in his brief span. In the end all he is doing is rushing more rapidly toward the grave.'

The old man was growing maudlin and lost now in his memories of things tried and failed at in his life, perhaps. His eyes were closed again as if all of the strength had gone out of him. The interview was at an end, and Sandy decided to make his departure. As he turned toward the door, Skye's faint voice asked, 'What are you going to do now, Rivers?'

'I couldn't say, sir. This is as far as my planning went.'

'Stay around for a while if you like . . . unless you're afraid of meeting Amos Coyne when he returns.'

'Thank you. I'll do that, then. Will he return — Coyne, that is? If he has taken the proceeds from this year's cattle sale, why would he return?'

'The Sky Box is worth much more than he could possibly have pilfered from me, Rivers. He'll be back if he's able. He'll be back for Corrine.'

Sandy Rivers stepped out of the room, closing the door behind him silently. His mood was thoughtful, dark. Far from feeling relieved of his burden as he had expected, he was morose, glum. He had darkened an old man's last days, hours, and with Coyne having vanished, there was not even any sort of retribution achieved. He had done all that he meant to do and found that all of it was useless.

Just like Vincent Skye.

A shadowy figure appeared before

him, and he heard the rustle of heavy skirts approaching. Corrine had emerged from one of the other rooms along the hallway. 'Use the front door, will you?' she said. 'The cook's in the pantry, readying breakfast. He starts early, and I don't want you startling anyone.'

She led him then down the inner stairs, across what seemed to be Vincent Skye's office and into the living room. She opened the front door and let him out into the chill, starlit night as Sandy was consulting his mental clock. Even for the earliest-rising cook, it seemed far too early to start planning breakfast. It could not have been far past midnight, if that. As the door closed behind him, he saw three shadows detach themselves from the surrounding darkness and stride toward him. Their faces were grim, their intent deadly. Sandy silently cursed himself. He had made a simpleminded mistake once again: trusting a woman.

Even with the only light a starglow filtered through a low veil of thin clouds it didn't take long for the shadowy figures to take on form and substance as they approached Sandy. Two of the men he recognized not only by their faces, but by their clothing and builds as well. Jordy Cavett and Randall Chandler led the way with a third insubstantial figure following. This one was too small to be Amos Coyne, and Sandy did not recognize the man even though they had presumably all spent weeks on the trail together.

'What are you doing here?' Randall Chandler growled. He tugged at his long, ragged red mustache as he spoke.

'I work here, remember?'

'The trail drive is over, Rivers. You have no business on this ranch.'

'That's not what Vincent Skye said.'

'Skye?' Chandler said incredulously. He was nearer now and Sandy could see the doubt and challenge in his eyes.

'That's right. He invited me to stay around.'

'When was this?'

'Not more than a few minutes ago.'

The narrow-built Jordy Cavett spoke up for the first time. 'Randy, if old man Skye — '

'Shut up!' Randall Chandler commanded. 'Rivers is lying, and even if he isn't, what do we care? We came here to do a job, and we're going to do it.'

'I wouldn't,' Sandy said. His hand rested on the stag-horn butt of his .44 Colt.

'Go ahead and shoot,' Chandler scoffed. 'You'll bring twenty Sky Box hands on the run, and they will shoot you down if they don't hang you.'

Chandler was right, of course, but he could certainly shoot Chandler and probably one of the other two. But Chandler's menacing threat carried some weight. The Sky Box crew would certainly be drawn to the sound of the shots, and it would be Sandy Rivers that they went for. A lynching would be the probable result.

Sandy's moment of indecision allowed Chandler to strike first. He winged a right-handed punch from far outside and clipped Sandy's jaw, sending Rivers staggering backward. As if that were the sign for a snarling wolf pack to attack, the three men immediately swarmed on Sandy.

Chandler grunted with pleasure as he threw a second right-hand fist slamming against Sandy's temple. Sandy had let Jordy get too close as well, and now the narrow man slipped the revolver from Sandy's holster and flung it away before joining in on the fun.

Chandler was behind Sandy now, pinning his arms back and Jordy moved in to slam lefts and rights against Sandy's ribcage. But Jordy was a little too near. Sandy smashed his forehead against Jordy Cavett's face and the small man moved away with a howl, blood streaming from his nose. The battering did not stop. They were willing to take turns.

'Get him, Cox!' Cavett screamed, and the third man was on top of Sandy as well. Chandler still had Sandy's arms pinned behind him in a vise-like grip. It momentarily worked to Sandy's advantage. As Cox moved toward him, his shoulders squared, fists tightly bunched, Sandy rocked back against Randall Chandler's body and lifted his feet, kicking out with both boots, catching Cox squarely on the chest.

Clutching his heart, Cox staggered back and spun away, retching. Jordy Cavett was now ready for a second try and he clomped forward on heavy boots, his anger plain on his swarthy face by the light of the just-rising moon.

Sandy struggled against the bearlike grip of Chandler, kicked back with his boot heels, twice catching the man painfully on the shins. Chandler's grip was released slightly and Sandy twisted free, ducking under a wild punch thrown by Jordy Cavett. When Sandy had straightened up, he had his own fists clenched, ready now to give as good as he got.

The shotgun blast took them all by surprise.

Briefly the night was lighted by a brilliant red and blinding yellow flare of the gun's explosion. Sandy, in a crouch, turned his eyes toward the source of the explosive shot.

'That's enough recreation for one night, boys,' Nate Arbuckle said. 'I've still got another barrel loaded with double-ought buckshot if someone don't agree.'

Randall Chandler, cursing violently, led the exodus, as Sandy's three attackers faded back into the shadows, Jordy Cavett pausing briefly to bend over and snatch up his hat. Nate limped his way forward to look Sandy over.

'Hurt you much?' he asked.

'They got my ribs pretty good,' Sandy said, holding himself with one arm. 'I don't think they're broken though.'

'All right,' Nate replied. 'Then let's get out of here before the boys storm from the bunkhouse to find out what's happened.'

'What are you going to tell them if they do come?' Sandy asked, as he moved along as hunched from pain as the twisted Nate Arbuckle.

'I'll tell them that I saw the bear that killed old Duke and took a shot at it.'

Sandy only nodded. He was in no mood for conversation although Nate must be curious about what had happened inside the Skye house on that night. Sandy was having some trouble drawing a deep breath and he continued to hold his ribs as if that were doing him any good. Nearing the barn, Sandy said to the yard man, 'Any pile of straw you can scrape together will suit me for a place to lie down, Nate.'

Arbuckle said wryly, 'What did you think I had in mind? Offering you my bed?'

Sandy stifled a laugh, fearful of the pain it might cause. He was getting used to sleeping on hay, he reflected. Then again it beat sleeping on open ground as he had during the long drive to the trail-head.

'I picked this up,' Nate said, handing Sandy his revolver. 'It might help you to sleep a little more easily. You should have used it in the first place.'

'Next time I will,' Sandy promised, meaning it.

Lowering himself onto the pile of hay provided by Nate Arbuckle was painfully slow, and sleep did not come easily on this cold night. But it came and Sandy Rivers was able to escape from the pain and uncertainty concerning his mission for a few blessed hours.

★　★　★

Morning was a muted yellow-orange light shining through the open barn doors into Sandy Rivers's face. He sat up on his bed of straw, started to stretch and found it sent pain darting through his ribcage. Nate was already up, obviously, since the tall twin doors of the barn were swung wide, but Sandy did not see the crooked man around.

Rising, Sandy stood for a minute leaning against a stall partition, trying to loosen the kinks in his body. He stopped at the red roan's stall briefly; patted the trail-weary Cookie's neck in passing, and then walked to the front doors. She was there, waiting patiently.

Corrine Skye sat on a white mare with a gray mane and tail, dressed in riding clothes — a divided buck-skin skirt and white blouse and jacket matching her skirt. A black, flat-crowned Spanish-style hat completed her costume.

'Do you always rise this late?' she asked. Her blue eyes were impenetrable. She held a silver-mounted riding crop in one hand. Her voice was vaguely antagonistic.

'No,' Sandy answered. 'Are you always up and riding this early?'

'As seldom as possible,' Corrine said. 'This morning I found it necessary.' Sandy raised an inquisitive eyebrow and waited. 'Father died during the night,' she said finally. There was only a momentary flash of anger and of sorrow in her eyes. Then her composure returned.

'I'll be riding with you,' she announced, and Sandy blinked into the sunlight.

'Who said I was riding anywhere?'

'You can't help us out on the ranch. I already had Nate and a couple of the boys take Father out to be buried. You, of course will be riding down Amos Coyne.' Her expression hardened as she asked, 'Or do I have to do the job on my own?'

It was all too much for Sandy to take in immediately. The girl had just seen her father pass away and yet, instead of mourning, she had simply called for a few of the ranch hands to dispose of him. Now she seemed intent on finding Amos Coyne, and she seemed smugly confident that Sandy Rivers was willing to go along with her.

'Won't your father need — ?'

'Vincent Skye no longer needs anything — except vengeance, or maybe that is my own concept. Rivers, I have been at my father's bedside, mourning him for many months. As to a funeral — he would have wanted to be buried on the ranch, his ranch. Some day I may manage to get a headstone for his grave. Right now there is nothing worth doing that I can do.'

She went on, 'I think the final straw was when you told him that Amos Coyne must have ridden off with the profit from the year's cattle sale. That is why I kept arguing against that possibility with you as well as taking Coyne's side in his treatment of the men. I just didn't want Father to hear what I had suspected for a long time. Bobo talked to me as well as to Father, you know.

'But, you see, my father had that dread feeling that everything he had worked for his entire life might be lost. That I would be left alone and helpless. He had misplaced all of his hopes for Sky Box and for me in Amos Coyne, believing that Coyne would continue to run and build up Sky Box. Hearing from you that Coyne had likely taken the year's profits and run off with them . . . '

'I'm sorry, then,' Sandy said. 'I would not have intentionally done anything to hurry the old man's demise.'

'No, I know that. Father just gave up his dreams in the middle of the night, and when a man is forced to do that, a man in his condition . . . He would have learned all sooner or later, Rivers. None of it is your doing except that you felt an obligation to your trail mates. You were trying to do what was right.

'Now!' she asked. 'Will you help *me* do what is right, or not?'

'Track down Amos Coyne, you mean?'

'That is exactly what I mean,' Corrine said, tossing her head. 'I intend to follow him anyway. On my own if necessary. But two on the trail are always safer than a lone rider, and you have as much reason to want to run him down as I do.'

Did he? Rivers considered. The young woman had lost a year's profits and her father, both of which might cripple the Sky Box dangerously. He had witnessed the killing of a man whom he did not particularly like back in Durant and suffered with Bob Bodine along the trail back. Otherwise all he was out was a gray horse he liked very much but which belonged to Sky Box anyway.

Did he want to track down Amos Coyne as much as the girl? No. He had considered his task completed after speaking with Vincent Skye. He was no bounty hunter, no lawman, not even some loyal long-time Sky Box hand. Looking up at the mounted woman, he could think of only one reason for continuing this mad pursuit.

That is, the way that the reckless Coyne had scarred Corrine's life even to depriving her of her father and possibly of Sky Box, the only home she had ever known, of her future. He supposed that was enough reason for any man to ride along with her. Where had he been heading anyway, he asked himself? Nowhere, was the answer. The rest of his life seemed to be a fading trail that ended nowhere in particular. He nodded his head.

'I'll get my horse and gear,' Sandy agreed.

'You have had no breakfast,' Corrine said. 'Put these in your saddle-bags.' And she handed him two thickly made roast beef sandwiches wrapped in waxed paper and four hard-boiled eggs. 'And make sure your canteen is full!' she added, as he turned away.

Sandy couldn't help himself. He rather sarcastically replied, 'Yes, boss!'

Then he started on into the barn. He saw Nate Arbuckle arrive with a dirt-caked shovel across his hunched shoulder. Arbuckle and Corrine muttered together for a while, and Sandy thought he heard a sob escape from the girl's lips.

'Ready for a little exercise?' Sandy said to the red roan, as he squeezed into the stall beside it. He smiled as he placed the thick sandwiches and hard eggs into his saddle-bags, and began to outfit the sleek red roan. Well, he was thinking, this is more than I started out with last time.

7

'Riding out with the lady, are you?' Nate Arbuckle asked, as Sandy was tightening the cinches on his saddle.

'She has a way of asking that makes it kind of hard to refuse,' Sandy answered.

'Yeah, well . . . watch out for her. And for yourself,' Nate said. 'Here's something you might need.' He handed Sandy a recognizable green box of .44 cartridges. 'Here's hoping you don't need them all.'

'There's always hope,' Sandy replied. Stuffing the .44s into the saddle-bags as well, he swung aboard the roan and walked the eager animal out into the brilliant morning sunlight. Sitting upright in his saddle was enough to make Sandy wince with the pain it caused his battered ribs, but Corrine seemed not to notice. She did notice his face, however.

'You've got a couple of nice bruises

on your face. I didn't notice those last night. What happened?'

She seemed innocent of the attack that Sandy had suffered after leaving her house. Perhaps it was only coincidence that she had instructed him to leave by the front door. Randall, Cavett and Cox might have been waiting out there because they naturally expected him to leave that way.

Sandy hoped so. He didn't like to think he might be riding into a deceitful woman's further plots. He could tell nothing by her face. There was no expression there except one of determination.

He had no idea how she expected to render justice to Amos Coyne and his friends. He asked her, 'How do you expect to do anything against these men?'

'They wouldn't dare lift a finger against me,' she said with certainty.

Now that might have been true back on Sky Box where they all worked for Vincent Skye, but this was a different situation. He asked her why she hadn't summoned her crew of cowboys to trail after Coyne, and it was explained — to her satisfaction — that they needed their working men on the ranch. This quest was her own idea; she couldn't pull valuable men away from their duties.

Which left Sandy, who apparently was not to be considered a valuable hand. Well, the woman was partly right. Sandy did still hold a grudge against Coyne although he felt that his part of the bargain had been achieved. He had told Vincent Skye of Amos Coyne's wicked ways. That was all he had felt obligated to do. Now the slim, erect lady riding next to him expected him to do more: to risk laying down his life for her and the Sky Box. Since he was employed by neither it seemed a large request. Just as puzzling was why Corrine should have enough faith in him to select him for this task. Surely among the ranch hands were one or two who could have been chosen to make the ride with her.

Maybe she figured that any man crazy enough to make the long ride Sandy had to warn her father was crazy enough or angry enough to continue pursuing Amos Coyne. Her words, her expression gave him no hint, and Sandy knew that he was not bright enough to understand the workings of a woman's mind.

'Can you find their trail?' Corrine asked.

'I have no idea where they're going,' he admitted. 'But three of Coyne's men were at the house last night . . . ' He paused, watching for some indication that Corrine had already known that. There was none. Her eyes were fixed straight ahead on the long land, her jaw set. 'Their tracks will be fresh and you'd think they have to be riding to meet Coyne.'

'And you haven't been able to pick up their sign yet?' Corrine asked.

'I've been looking; but not yet.' Sandy shook his head. 'Let's angle northward a little. We're bound to cut their sign if they came this way, which they must have; they wouldn't hit the long trail back to La Paloma — and there is no other place to go in that direction.'

Corrine nodded and remained silent as the dawn-red sun rose higher and yellowed. It wasn't long before they did cut the fresh sign of three horses heading westward into the low foothills. To be certain, Sandy asked, 'Should there be any Sky Box men riding this way this morning?'

'No, of course not,' Corrine said, as if Sandy were a fool for asking.

'I just wanted to be sure,' he answered, his voice a little cranky. 'I wouldn't want to waste the morning following a false trail.'

They had drawn up near a shallow creek, glittering a silver-blue in the early sunlight.

Corrine asked, 'If we find Amos Coyne's tracks, how would we know?'

'How?' Sandy had removed his hat to

wipe out the sweat band with his kerchief. 'We might not for sure. I'm not familiar with his horse's prints. I never had reason to pay any particular attention to them. But from what we know, we should see signs of a lone rider leading three stolen horses.'

'Like these?' Corrine asked, her eyes sharp and clear. She pointed to the mud flanking the creek. Sandy swung down to study the tracks. Separated, but not widely from those of the three men they had been following, there were definite hoofprints of a gathering of ponies, led to water at this point. In the softer soil they had lasted quite a while. Sandy squatted down on his heels and studied them more closely.

'Was I right?' Corrine said, her glow triumphant as Sandy swung back into leather.

'You were right,' Sandy nodded. For in the soft earth he had seen the prints of a horse newly shod on its front hoofs. They were the tracks of his own stolen gray horse.

Corrine rode with Sandy across the shallow creek, her eyes still bright with a sort of pleasure. But as they rose from the far side of the bottom and started onward toward the long row of distant hills again and the sun continued to rise and grow warmer, as the miles passed those eyes faded to weary resignation. Finding Amos Coyne's sign was not the same as catching up with the turncoat, running him down and recovering the stolen money from the cattle sale which was needed not only for present debts and future operations, but for paying the men who now rode for Sky Box.

Corrine had a lot to consider and to worry about, and all of Sky Box's problems were now hers alone. Once, as the long trail continued to wind on and the day grew hotter, Sandy glanced at the woman whose mouth formed a few silent sounds which might have been curses aimed at Amos Coyne. Well, she had every right.

Approaching the ragged, broken foothills in mid-afternoon, at Sandy's suggestion they decided to look for a shady place to rest. The horses were flagging and their lungs were heated and filled with trail dust, their throats parched. Coyne and his crew would have stopped as well during the heat of the day. There would have been no point in them running hard when they expected no pursuit. Sandy and Corrine would not be losing much ground to them by resting for a while.

Or so Sandy had convinced himself. His back, ribs and shoulders were aching and his head was throbbing. He had to get out of the saddle for at least a little while. The red roan was an easy-riding horse, but its every step now sent a jolt of pain through Sandy's skull.

'Do you see anything?' Corrine asked, surveying the empty land ahead of them, her own weariness plain.

'Just ahead, a small stand of live-oak trees. See them?'

They swung down in the shelter of four or five dusty trees which did little to cut the harsh afternoon sunlight angling through their branches. There was a patch of short yellow grass beneath the trees, brittle and also dusty. The horses did not seem to mind as they foraged for what nourishment they could find. Sandy removed the bandanna he had been wearing across his nose and mouth against the windblown dust and used it to wipe out his hat once again and to dry his neck and throat. He had always heard that women do not perspire as freely as men. He did not know why, but as Corrine removed her hat and sat on the dry earth as gracefully as if she were seating herself on some comfortable settee, her tanned face was dry and smooth-appearing.

Sandy lowered himself to the ground a little distance away from her. The movements employed caused the pain in his ribs and shoulders to begin acting up again. Corrine sat serenely studying the land around them. Sandy watched her blue eyes and the dark hair the wind grasped and teased, the fine lines of her cheeks and jaw.

'I think I know where they've gone,' Corrine announced suddenly, still keeping her eyes on the wide land, the tangle of the low rank of broken hills.

'You do?' Sandy asked with some surprise. He then took a drink of tepid water from his canteen and watched and waited for a full minute while Corrine considered.

'Yes, once, years ago when I still considered Amos Coyne to be a gentleman and a trustworthy man, he and I rode out this way. It was in the spring — much cooler, of course, with wildflowers scattered across the land. He began telling me of a section of grassland he had found south of Bigelow — do you know where that town is, Rivers?'

'I've been past it. If you don't have a good reason to stop there, there's no point in doing so.'

'Yes. I was given to understand that it was quite small, but growing.'

'It's malformed and I doubt it will

133

'ever grow,' Sandy replied, drawing a fairly sharp glance from Corrine.

'Just because you don't like Amos Coyne . . . ' She began again. 'Anyway, I was told that Bigelow was set to grow, it only needed more commerce brought in. Cattle ranches often bring prosperity to nearby towns.'

'So long as they've got a saloon and a female population,' Sandy agreed.

'Rivers,' Corrine scolded, 'you know you are difficult to talk to.'

'I suppose,' he answered. 'I do most of my talking to my horses and to trail-hardened men.' He paused. 'Usually I'm called Sandy, not Rivers, by the way.'

'By the horses?' Corrine asked teasingly, and she smiled. It was an irresistible expression and Sandy grinned in return. He was interested now in Bigelow and what Amos Coyne had indicated might be where he had planned to root his new ranch.

'Did you ever see the country he had in mind?' Sandy enquired.

'No,' the girl said, 'we never did get

that far on that day. It's a long ride, you understand, and if I was not home by sunset, Father would have skinned the both of us.'

'He was a wise man.'

'He was rough on me!' Corrine said sharply. 'Mean, you might say.'

Sandy asked softly, 'And aren't you glad now that he was?'

Corrine smiled again. 'Yes,' she said, nodding her head. 'Yes, I suppose I am.' She started to rise. 'Think the horses have had enough of a rest?'

'Not really, but I guess that's about all they need.' He stood, looking westward himself. The tracks they had been following earlier had long since faded out against the dry earth, too hard to take imprints. 'What do you think we should do, Corrine? Continue in the direction their tracks were tending or straightline it into Bigelow?'

'Bigelow, if it is up to me. We can find a place to eat and beds to sleep on. In the morning we can start fresh, and someone in the town will be able to give us instructions if Coyne is trying to bootstrap a new ranch around there.'

'Which he seems to be doing. Remember all the missing calves, the stolen horses. And he will have plenty of money now to go ahead with his grand plans.'

'Plenty of *my* money,' Corrine said fiercely as she swung aboard the white mare again. Sandy noted that she did not say 'my father's money'. Of course it was no longer Vincent Skye's, but it bothered Sandy a little. Sandy swung onto the roan's back, and as they started on their way across the dry-grass plain, he found himself wondering once again what it was that had Corrine so furious — the loss of her father, the theft of the money from the cattle drive, or perhaps something else?

Was there any possibility that she was enraged because Coyne had broken a trust, a promise to her, that as much as she denied it, there was still something between the two? The sun was still hot and high, the trail long and dusty; his body still ached from the beating he had taken the night before. Sandy Rivers turned his thoughts away from speculation and followed along toward the tiny, distant town of Bigelow, glancing only occasionally at the fine, firm face of the woman beside him, not neglecting to scour the empty land ahead, knowing that there could be men out there wishing to do them harm.

★ ★ ★

Bigelow was a shabby, misshapen monument to someone's lost ambition. None of the wooden buildings seemed able to hold itself erect and the entire town seemed to be slumping down, ready to sag into the earth and give up its battle for survival. Sandy and Corrine Skye had the time to take a good long look at it as they angled down a rounded hill where yellow and purple mustard flowers flourished and sumac stood in isolated clumps.

'It'll take more than a few cattle to revive this patient,' Sandy commented, as he guided the red roan in that direction.

'It is a rather dismal-looking sight, isn't it?' Corrine was forced to agree. 'But look at the town of Durant. There's nothing to keep it alive but that railroad spur and the cattle that are driven in to the trail head.'

'There's no way they will ever construct a spur out to this isolated shack-town. The country's too rough, and there's no need for it anyway.'

'A flourishing ranch can support a small town,' Corrine believed. 'That may be what these people are counting on.' She smiled faintly. 'I don't know why else anyone would stay here.'

They had reached the flats and started along what might have been considered a road leading into Bigelow. What it was, was a set of wagon wheel ruts worn deep by constant travel. No wagoner would try to drive outside of them: there would be the constant threat of slipping in and breaking a wheel or axle. And so the ruts grew deeper. As they drew nearer the road became muddy although it had not rained in weeks.

'Must be underground springs somewhere,' Sandy commented.

'That would explain why someone would build here.'

'Yeah. Keep your eyes open, Corrine,' he said as they entered the town proper, riding slowly between opposing ranks of rough-timbered buildings.

'For a hotel, you mean?'

'For familiar horses,' he said a little roughly. 'You know? Four-legged animals sporting a Sky Box brand on their flanks.'

'You don't have to get grouchy with me,' Corrine scolded. 'I'm tired, that's all. My first thoughts were on finding a place out of the saddle to rest.'

'Sorry,' Sandy muttered, and he was, even if he didn't sound like it. Corrine was a fine horsewoman, but unlike Sandy she had never spent days and nights on horseback over rough country. And, Sandy reflected honestly, there had been times when sleeping on rough, rocky ground that he would have given a month's pay to lie down on an actual mattress. 'I didn't mean to be rough on you. I guess I'm near as tired as you are. Let's find a place to put up our horses, then we'll start looking around.'

'What if there is no hotel?' Corrine asked with some trepidation, as she looked at the dreary, weather-beetled fronts of the slump-shouldered buildings they passed.

'Someone will give us a place to sleep for a few dollars.' He glanced at her, apologetic and hopeful at once. 'You must have a few dollars with you, at least.'

'Father taught me never to go anywhere completely broke, even if all the money you could carry was what you had stuffed in your boot. And you're working for me, Sandy, remember? Don't worry about paying our way.'

Father had been right, of course, but

it must have been many years ago, if ever, that Vincent Skye had been as flat broke as Sandy was just then. Corrine had probably never gone without anything she needed. Sandy muttered a quiet thanks for wealthy girls. They had just passed a restaurant. Although they had seen no sign on the building, the scents of hearty cooking were unmistakable. Sandy's stomach rumbled. The roast beef sandwiches and hard-boiled eggs were only a memory now.

The stable was easy enough to find. It sat on the far left-hand side of the street, fifty yards or so from the nearest building. An unseen horse whickered a welcome. Sandy helped a weary Corrine from the saddle and led the horses into the dimness of the building. A small man, bouncy as a rubber ball and almost as round, came out to meet them. Sandy took him for a Portuguese, but could not swear to it. It made no difference anyway.

The stablehand wore a broad, flourishing black mustache and a wide white smile. 'Hello, hello, gentleman and lady. I am at your service.'

'Fine. We just want to put the horses up overnight. Give them oats if you have them.'

'Oh, I have them,' the little man said, running a hand along the roan's flank. 'I see a Rocking R, huh?' he said, indicating the brand. Stablehands had an intense interest in the brands on the horses they were given. They were a kind of travel guide to them.

'Far from home range,' Sandy said. 'I've had him for a long time, and we've done some traveling over the years.'

'Oh, yes,' the man said, his eyes bright as if happy to have that bit of information. He shifted his attention to the white horse Corrine rode. He traced the brand with his finger. 'Now, this one I do not know,' he admitted.

'It's Sky Box,' Corrine said as if slightly offended. 'We're not very far from here.'

'Yes — but no one rides to Bigelow, I think.'

'Not much reason to is there?' Corrine asked a little sharply. Then she cooled, looking ashamed of her outburst.

Sandy enquired, 'So you haven't seen any other Sky Box branded horses in town?'

'No, sir,' the man said, still smiling widely. 'I would have seen. I see them all. This is a very new, strange brand to me.'

When they left the stable, Corrine was still huffing as if piqued that Sky Box wasn't as well known in the territory as she had assumed. Corrine had grown up there, saw it every day of her life; they shipped hundreds of cattle every year. To her it was the center of the world. It's sometimes difficult for people to come to grips with the fact that their own world is a little smaller, of less importance than they had believed.

'Well, we know that Amos Coyne and his crew haven't been in Bigelow,' Sandy said as they rapidly walked across the street toward the heart of town.

'We only know that they haven't been keeping their horses in that stable,' Corrine said logically as they stepped up onto a sagging boardwalk.

'You're right,' Sandy agreed. 'Where are we heading now?'

The sky was darkening. A cool breeze had risen with the day's ending. The hunched little town seemed to surround them and sag toward them, the sad old faces of its buildings watching them. The tired wood of the plankwalk was spongy under their boots.

'I'm hungry, and you must be as well,' Corrine said. 'Let's eat and find a place to sleep, continue on in the morning.'

'Into the Valley of Death?' Sandy asked lightly.

'To wherever that thieving, skulking coyote has his lair!'

8

You don't expect the food to be much in a place like Bigelow. Maybe we have the idea that good food takes an accompanying fancy décor like expensive restaurants try to convince us. The breakfast Corrine and Sandy had shared that morning was among the best either could remember. Supper the night before had been beyond delight. If the cook had been working somewhere other than Bigelow, Colorado, her fortune would have been made.

'I've found a reason to live in Bigelow,' Sandy said, as they stepped out onto the plankwalk to relish the warm morning sunlight.

'I'd hire her,' Corrine agreed.

'Can't you cook?' Sandy asked.

'Not like that!' Corrine admitted.

'Oh, well,' Sandy said carelessly. 'Since I have to choose between you,

I'll take the cook.'

'Did you get a good look at her?'

'What's a hundred pounds or so between friends?'

'Besides,' Corrine said more seriously, 'any choosing you have to do does not include me, Mr Rivers. I am not on the auction block.'

'Well enough,' Sandy muttered, throwing his toothpick away. 'I couldn't afford you anyway.'

'No. You probably couldn't afford the cook, either, and I doubt you could charm her into it. None of you saddle tramps is as charming as you believe yourselves to be.'

On that note they started on their way again, recovering their horses from the Portuguese's stable, heading out with the sun on their right, the broken hills ahead and the dying little town of Bigelow behind them.

'A puppy,' Corrine heard Sandy say as they crested a hill rise.

'What did you say, Mr Rivers?'

'I said I'd like to get a puppy after

146

we're married — I wonder if the cook likes dogs?'

'With onions and parsley,' Corrine answered. She was able to control her smile long enough for Sandy's grin to reappear.

'You're probably right. Let's go bag us some coyotes instead.' After a minute of silent riding, he asked seriously, 'Corrine, have you given any thought as to how we're going to pull this off? Ride right in and tell Coyne to give you your father's money back? Is that the idea?'

'He'll have to give it to me,' Corrine said definitely. 'If he doesn't, he'll be ruined in these parts, branded as a thief. I'll bring twenty-five men with me and threaten to hang Amos and all of his filthy crew. I might even do it,' she added.

'That's fine — in your imagination,' Sandy told her. 'Except I don't think that Amos Coyne gives a hoot about his reputation so long as he is making money. As for bringing in a gang of Sky

Box riders, just how are we supposed to tell them they are needed if he doesn't let us go once he has his hands on us?'

'You don't understand anything, do you, Rivers?'

'Maybe not,' Sandy said with a shrug. 'I thought I did. I thought I knew what kind of man Amos Coyne is.'

'Amos would never, ever harm me,' Corrine said with confidence. 'He would not dare! I'll tell him how things must be and even allow him to keep the stolen horses and the cattle, if he truly has them, until such time as he can afford to pay me back. All on paper, of course. I will help him start his ranch, but make it clear that he must return the receipts from Sky Box's cattle sale to me.' She spoke this all with serious conviction. Had the girl been raised in such a sheltered environment that she actually believed her plan could succeed, that Amos Coyne, her disappointed suitor, respected, admired her enough to follow her conditions?

One of them, at least, had no

148

understanding of what they were getting themselves into, and Sandy Rivers doubted that it was him. That didn't make him the smarter of the two. Corrine was going to visit the killer in blissful unawareness. Sandy was riding along with her because . . . He glanced at her fine profile and at the splendid figure she made in the saddle . . .

He continued to ride with Corrine because he was a plain fool.

Ahead the trail crested on a knoll where stacks of yellow-white boulders lined the way. Reaching the summit they were able to look down on a pretty little valley. There was a stone house and a pole corral where a dozen or so hires were penned. They could see a herd of white-faced cattle grazing their patient way across the land. Sandy noted a stack of sawn lumber with a gray tarpaulin thrown carelessly over it beside the house.

'He's been at this for some time,' Sandy commented.

'Yes, it seems to be thriving,' Corrine

answered. 'I think we were meant to live here whether Amos took control of Sky Box or not.' She was leaning forward in her saddle, both hands braced against the pommel as she peered downward. Perhaps sensing Sandy's eyes on her she quickly added, 'Not that I would have ever married Amos Coyne, of course — but I think he intended to show me what he could do.'

'I think with enough stolen money and stock anyone could have done this,' Sandy said, irrationally irritated by Corrine's comments. Where was the girl's heart at, actually? She seemed to be ready to lynch Coyne at one minute and admiring of him the next. Perhaps old bonds still held sway.

'We should start on down,' Corrine said.

'Yes,' a strange voice said from behind a low clump of rocks. 'That is exactly what you should do, Miss Skye, but do us the favor of shedding your guns first, Rivers.'

The gravelly vice belonged to Randall

Chandler. He tugged at his bushy red mustache after emerging from behind the rocks, rifle in hand, with the diminutive Jordy Cavett following. Cavett's face, Sandy noted, was still bruised from their last encounter. His small dark eyes were fierce with hatred.

Corrine was incensed. 'Since you know who I am, you have no cause to treat us like this. I have come to visit Amos Coyne. Mr Rivers is my escort. I won't have my own employees acting like roughnecks!'

'We kinda forgot to tell you that we've quit Sky Box,' Chandler said, with a sly edge to his voice. 'It don't matter much what you think any more, Miss Skye. Shed those guns, Rivers!'

Corrine was not finished. 'I'll have twenty men down on you in a flash!' she warned Chandler.

'Yes, miss,' Chandler drawled, looking down the slope behind them. 'And who exactly is going to go tell them that you need help?'

Sandy had unsheathed his Winchester

and handed it over gently to the scowling Jordy Cavett. Now he unholstered his Colt and reversed it to slap it into Cavett's hand. There was no point in starting a war he could not win.

Corrine continued in an angry voice. 'I demand to see Amos Coyne. Ruffians such as you should have no place on this ranch!'

Cavett seemed to shrink a little. Having lost his job on Sky Box, he could not afford to make his new boss angry. Randall Chandler took her words more lightly. He lowered the muzzle of his Winchester and smiled faintly.

'Oh, you'll be seeing Coyne all right, Miss Skye. We'll make sure of that.' Over his shoulder he instructed Cavett, 'Grab our ponies, Jordy. Let's escort these visitors to the house.'

With one of the outlaw Sky Box riders on either side of them, Corrine and Sandy made their way down the grassy slope toward the bootstrap ranch that sat on the valley floor. Corrine rode with her head held high, her eyes straight ahead. Sandy watched their guards for signs of inattention or carelessness even though it would make no difference if he could find a way to disarm one of the men or to spur his horse away from their watching eyes.

No, he decided, he would not try anything. There was nothing to be gained, no point in it. Did he want shots fired wildly with Corrine in the midst of things? What would escaping gain him? He would still have to find a way to rescue Corrine — if she even wished to be rescued.

As they approached the stone house, she still rode with apparent confidence in her own ability to handle Amos Coyne. Sandy Rivers did not share that confidence.

He noticed that the windows in the newly built house had not been fitted with glass — a hard to come by item this far out on the plains, but that wrought-iron bars bent at a ninety-degree angle at either end had been set into the mortar between the stones in the walls, making it as secure as any jail. Except that in this case the jailer had chosen to dwell within himself. Was Amos Coyne that fearful? Of what, of whom?

They came up to a white-painted hitch rail, newly put in place and, as Corrine swung nimbly down from her white mare, Randall Chandler's rifle muzzle was kept trained on Rivers.

'You stay where you are,' Chandler told him. 'She might be a guest, but you're not. We've got another place for you.'

And Corrine did seem to be a welcome guest. Before they turned away, Sandy saw the heavy plank door to the stone house open and he recognized Amos Coyne with his brushed-back dark hair and emotionless black eyes standing there. He and Corrine greeted each other, not exactly with an embrace, but each took the other's arms for a moment, and then Corrine was escorted into the house's interior, the door closing solidly behind her.

'Seen enough?' Chandler asked.

'I suppose so,' Sandy answered in a muffled voice. Enough to cause him to think that he was among the fools of all time; even though he did not understand what game was being played, it was obvious that he was odd man out.

The outbuilding where they took Sandy, roughly dragging him from the saddle and throwing him inside, was built along lines similar to Coyne's house. Gray stone with iron bars across the windows which were, anyway, too small for a grown man to wriggle through. The building, no more than twenty feet square, reeked of tallow, slag, oil and kerosene. There was a rusted plow in one corner, a nail keg, a set of hand tools, empty jugs and stacks of sacking. All without plan, just items variously collected and stored to be used or disposed of another time. Sandy moved about in the near-darkness, the only light in the room coming from a pair of head-high ten-inch wide windows.

In one corner he discovered three new branding irons. Their heads formed a

Circle C. For Coyne, no doubt. The man was serious about starting his own ranch. He had all the necessary beginnings . . . thanks to Vincent Skye. Probably Coyne had developed his idea as it became obvious that Skye was no longer capable of a trail drive, of surveying his ranch to see what mischief Coyne might be up to.

Then Coyne had suddenly made a grab for a big payday, stealing the receipts from the cattle sale. Why? To accelerate his building programme, no doubt. Perhaps he still owed someone money for the land and wanted to clear the debt. Now, when Vincent Skye had become bedridden, would have been the time to take the gamble. Skye was not going to rise from his bed and track Coyne down. And Corrine? What reason did Amos Coyne have to fear her?

Sandy picked up a few of the hand tools — a saw, a claw hammer, a drill bit. None of them were of any use to a man seeking to find a way out of a

156

stone house. There was a jug of kerosene, but nothing to burn but the heavy plank door. Even had the shed been made of wood, Sandy would not have tried that trick. He couldn't think of a more futile way to go than to be trapped inside a burning building by a fire he had started himself.

He seated himself on the pile of sacking — burlap bags left from oats that had been delivered to the ranch. With his arms looped abound his knees he studied the room again. It had no floor. Probably it had been constructed before Coyne had come by the lumber Sandy had seen. But the earth was packed solidly. Sandy figured that with the right tools he could have dug himself out in a week or so.

He doubted he would have that long to ponder the situation.

He heard a sharp, short laugh and got to his feet. It was a woman's laugh he had heard, and walking to one of the narrow barred windows, he saw that he had a clear view into one of the rooms inside Coyne's house. There he saw two shadowy figures — Coyne and Corrine Skye — standing close together and discussing something. Corrine laughed again and Sandy turned away from the window feeling betrayed and a little bit sick to his stomach.

In Sunday school hadn't there been something abut the tongue of a lying woman being sharper than a serpent's tooth? He couldn't remember exactly how that went, but he saw what the old-timer had been talking about.

Why him? Why had Corrine roped him into this crazy expedition? Was it because he was the only man on the Sky Box who was ignorant of her ways and was the easiest to convince? Or had she just known that he was born a fool? Why had Sandy agreed to come at all?

That was the easiest question. That fine trim figure, those brilliant blue eyes, her silken dark hair and beautiful smile could take the blame for that. He had once stumbled into a women's meeting where the speaker was proclaiming that when they got the vote they would have some power in this country. She obviously didn't get around much. When did women not have power over men?

Driving away the useless thoughts from his mind Sandy seated himself again and tried to think of nothing. What was there to think about? He could not plan an escape, had no idea what he would do if he could get out of the storage shack, had no idea on how he could contribute to Corrine's plan — if she even had one — or what it was.

He wondered bitterly if Turk Bemis and Jerry Higgins hadn't gotten the better part of the bargain they had made back in Durant.

* * *

It was in the hour before sunset that Amos Coyne appeared in the doorway, his bullwhip coiled in his hand, his dark hair brushed back, his dark eyes coldly furious. Sandy, who had been dozing in misery, immediately came to his feet. The sky beyond Coyne was faintly colored; he was a bulky dark silhouette before it. He slapped his leg with the coiled whip and took two strides into the shed.

'I know what you're up to, Rivers,' Coyne said in his easy baritone voice. Many men had taken that voice to be soothing, kindly; Sandy knew that it covered a lot of venom.

'Good. Tell me then,' Sandy replied, 'because I have no idea what I'm up to.'

'So you're a jokester,' Coyne said.

'That's what I'm up to?' Sandy asked, managing a grin. As he answered, Sandy saw the man's fingers loosen, and the bullwhip uncoil at his feet like a dying snake. Coyne took anther step forward, leading his whip. There was no one to be seen behind him, but Sandy would have wagered that he was not alone.

'You just can't stay out of things, can you? I saw you with Bobo out on the desert. Now this,' Coyne said, shaking his head as if with sadness. Sorry he had to whip his dog for getting into the garbage.

'Now this, what?' Sandy exclaimed. 'What am I into now? I don't even know why you've got such an itch to lash me — and that is your intent, isn't it?'

'It is my intent,' Coyne answered in his nice baritone voice, as if he truly regretted it and not because he was a sadistic bastard who felt that if he let a day go by without using his whip on some animal, man, woman or child it had been a wasted day.

Sandy, half-crouched, made his plan. When he saw the muscles in Coyne's arms flinch, he would step forward, grab the whip and yank hard. Then he would move in, going at Coyne with knees, feet, fists and skull.

It was a nice plan — in imagination. Coyne's wrist flicked and braided black leather lashed Sandy's arm. The bite of the whip was as heavy and brutal as being struck by a massive timber rattler.

The whip tore away flesh as Coyne

yanked back. Its tip had been fitted with razor-sharp bits of metal. Stunned by the swiftness of the first lash of the bull-whip, Sandy staggered away and froze momentarily. That was long enough for Amos Coyne to strike again.

The blacksnake whip snapped again, and Sandy had enough time to turn away, shielding his face with his forearms. He had the idea that Coyne, if he had a mind to, could pluck out his eyeballs with that damnable weapon. There was no hiding from the whip — a bullet might even have been dodged, but the bullwhip did not care where it struck as it made its murderous arc, and its loop was wide.

The whip wound around Sandy's body, the steel hooks at its tip biting into the flesh of his ribs and abdomen, unwinding with a jerk of Coyne's arm to make its bloody way across Sandy's back, drawing angry furrows across his flesh. Hot blood began to seep from Sandy's torso, front and back, and there was no way to fight back. Sandy found himself slumping to his knees, his forearms still in front of his eyes.

Peering up, Sandy could see Amos Coyne's face — it was dark and expressionless. There was nothing at all, neither hatred nor triumph in his eyes. As Sandy watched, the man recoiled the whip into neat dark loops.

'That'll give you something to think about,' Coyne said, as he pushed open the plank door behind him. Then, to one of the men outside the shack, 'Jordy, the man must be hungry. Bring him a cup of that bean soup we have on the stove.'

The door closed, leaving Sandy crouched and beaten in the near-darkness. Why hadn't Coyne killed him if that was what he had wanted, when he had the chance? Reflecting, Sandy realized that Coyne had never actually flogged a man to death with his whip. Not Bob Bodine, and not Len Storch, who had finally been done in by a knife in the back, not the lash of Coyne's whip.

Was that some primitive principle of Coyne's? Maybe the fun went out of the sadism after a man was down and no longer able to register fear or feel the bite of the lash. Sandy only knew that he was alive, for now, and if he could do anything to stop it, he would never allow himself to be whipped again.

Now! he thought suddenly. Now was his best chance to escape. Jordy Cavett had been sent to the kitchen to fetch soup for Sandy — why, Sandy could not guess. Another of Coyne's primitive rules? Perhaps the gesture was meant to be a show of civility for his guest.

What had he told Corrine as he went out with his whip? That he was just going to check to see that Sandy was comfortable, that he regretted locking the cowboy in the shed but that he mistrusted Sandy's motives for coming here? Some such tale, Sandy decided. Coyne would have his story all worked out — he had demonstrated to be a long-time, proficient liar.

Sandy's problem now was to get out

of the shed, to escape free into the night where he would have the time to consider what was to be done about rescuing Corrine — who did not seem to feel that she needed rescuing.

He rose to his feet, his body feeling bruised. Blood continued to seep into his shirt. His head was dizzy and his vision fogged with pain. No matter. He was never going to have a better chance to escape, and he eased up beside the heavy, outward-swinging door, the bone-handled knife he had been carrying in his leather vest clenched in his bloody hand.

9

'Come on, you little bastard,' Sandy was muttering as he waited, dripping blood, beside the door. After what seemed to be hours, he heard the approach of boots. Sandy strained to hear more clearly. One man's boots or two? Would Jordy have been sent over by himself? It seemed imprudent, but then perhaps Coyne had believed the fight had been whipped out of Sandy Rivers, and envisioned him curled up in a ball in the corner of the shack, whimpering like a beaten dog.

No matter. Jordy Cavett was at the door, unlocking it. The door swung open away from Sandy and Jordy entered cautiously, carrying a large steaming mug in one hand. His other rested on his holstered Colt. A mistake. He should have drawn the pistol before entering. Not that it would have deterred Sandy, who was in a hot rage and probably would have charged the muzzle of a Colt .44.

As it was, Cavett nudged the door open with his elbow, peered uncertainly into the darkness of the shed and felt his wrist being grabbed, yanked forward and before the little man could react he was standing with Sandy's arm crooked around his throat, the point of the bone-handled knife prodding him under his chin. The cup with the steaming bean soup had dropped to the ground as Cavett pawed uselessly at his holstered weapon.

'You hold still, Jordy,' Sandy's voice, rough in the darkness, whispered into his ear, 'or you're done. Do you understand?'

'What do you want?' Jordy asked, his voice high and trembling.

'I've got it,' Sandy said, slipping the Colt revolver from Jordy's rig. 'The question is what do you want? I don't figure I've got the time to tie and gag you properly. I'm leaving now, and you're

staying. See that window right there?'
Sandy asked with seeming irrelevance,
and Jordy nodded his head as best he
could with Sandy's arms still tightly around
his throat.

'It's just the right height for shooting
through, and if I hear a peep out of you
before I'm ready to make my move, I'll
be at that window to tell you goodbye
with your Colt.'

'Coyne will — ' Jordy said shakily.

'Make up your mind if you're willing
to die for Coyne, Jordy. I don't have the
time to wait.'

The knife point was pressed a little
more strongly against Jordy's throat.
He was afraid to nod again. A hissing
whisper came through his teeth.

'I won't make a sound.'

Not that Sandy trusted the man to keep
his word, but he sounded frightened
enough to remain silent for a few minutes at least and that was all he needed.
Sandy shoved Jordy away from him roughly,
watching the small man trip and fall to
the ground. In demonstration, Sandy

lowered the muzzle of the Colt in Jordy's direction and slipped out into the silent darkness of the night, closing the door behind him as silently as possible.

Pressed against the stone wall of the outbuilding, Sandy looked around for moving shadows. Randall Chandler seemed never to be far away from Jordy, and Kent Cox must still be working for Coyne although he had not seen Cox since his arrival. There may have been other men as well. Probably were. Someone must have been left behind to watch the ranch while Coyne was gone. These would be out now riding night herd, a necessary job. Coyne would have cowhands out on the range. He was a thieving, sadistic brute, but he was a cattleman.

There were still lanterns lighted in the house and muted voices could be heard. There was a temptation to look through one of the barred windows to try seeing Corrine. That urge was overcome by the knowledge that anyone who happened to glance his way was liable to shoot his head off.

And Jordy's resolve to remain silent would be fading. By now he would figure that Sandy had made his escape and if he wanted to keep his job it was in his best interests to raise the alarm.

Sandy decided that it was in his own best interests to hightail it out of there.

Where he was going was, of course, the first question. His impulse was to break into Coyne's house, but there would be armed men in there — and he was not sure at this point if Corrine even wanted to be rescued from Coyne's clutches. Away, then, somewhere where he could rest for a bit and formulate a plan while keeping an eye on the house. The layout of the ranch was pretty clear in his mind. There were stacks of boulders along the road coming in where a man could conceal himself. But by daylight he would find himself hot, thirsty and exposed.

Higher up the flanks of the surrounding hills were stands of pine trees which offered good shelter, but the climb up might prove to be too much for him, the shape he was in. Down in the valley bottom stood groves of scattered oak trees. There must be water there at least, but if there were, that was where the cattle would be herded, meaning men would be standing watch over them.

Sandy stood limply holding Jordy Cavett's pistol in one hand, uncertain and confused — the result of the lashing Coyne had given him, no doubt. His ribs still ached from the beating he had taken back on Sky Box and his arm where the lash had bitten was throbbing. His abdomen was still leaking blood, as was his back. His head ached miserably. He felt like a small animal that has escaped from its cage and now has no idea how to proceed. It was almost full dark now; there was only the faintest purple haze above the mountains and it was hours before the late moon would begin its eastern ascent.

Jordy Cavett began shouting from near the shed, and the front door of the house was thrown open, lantern light from within revealing two men rushing out onto the porch, rifles in their hands. Sandy took to his heels, running through the night at a staggering, uneven pace. He hadn't made it fifty yards before he had to halt for breath, bent over at the waist, holding his stomach. Back at the house there was some tumult, but most of it seemed to involve only shouting; no pursuit was mounted. In the darkness that would have been futile, anyway. They could not know which direction he had taken.

Probably Jordy Cavett would be assigned to stand watch all night on the front porch out of concern and retribution against the small man. When Sandy could breathe more easily again, he started on his way, moving toward the creek and the scattered oak trees along it. He needed a horse, first of all, and he had not even seen any near the house. Now, of course, he could not go back and look around. His next best choice, he reasoned, came with finding one of the cowhands riding night herd and stealing his horse. It was risky, and if shots were fired in the attempt, he could expect trouble. Still, he saw no good alternative. It was bad enough being afoot in the night; to be found that way when daylight came would leave Sandy Rivers with no way out, no hope of escape.

And where would he go if he could make his way off the ranch? Back to Sky Box to raise the alarm, tell the cowboys there that Corrine had been taken hostage? He refused to let himself think that far ahead. One step at a time. He needed a horse, badly needed one. A picture rose in his mind of a time not long ago of him, Turk and Jerry having finished a difficult job enjoying themselves quietly over beer in the saloon in Durant, celebrating their footloose status. Nothing to do, no one to please, no urgency in their small world to do anything at all. How had that come to this? A hunted man running through the tangled night trying to escape a sadistic dog of a man, his life only a false move from ending on this dark, unknown land.

He guessed that it was about an hour later when he reached the flats of the valley and slipped among the dark shadows of the oaks. Still, there had been no sounds of pursuit from behind him. Probably Coyne had decided that there was no point in chasing down the cowboy who could do nothing to stop him and his scheming. Or maybe Corrine had spoken up, telling the men to leave Sandy alone . . . he grinned at his own foolishness. The thought had brought a small moment of warm feeling, but was probably only wishful imagining.

Sandy worked his way carefully through the oak trees. He was now able to see the narrow creek shimmering with a vague silver gleam in the starlight. He heard cattle, but could not see them. They would be mostly bedded down now and would appear only as dark lumps against the darker ground.

He thought of waiting for the moon

to rise before he tried anything, but if the moon gave vision to him, it would also aid any searchers or patrolling riders. These men were his best chance, he realized. It was normal to circle the herd in the night. Some men hummed or whistled to quiet the herd, to assure the cattle that they were being watched. Some even sang tuneless cattle lullabies to announce themselves, or to calm their own nerves and alleviate the boredom of riding night herd. Whether the riders did any of these or remained silent, if Sandy could get nearer to the herd, sooner or later he would see one of these lonesome men passing by.

He went to the creek and crossed it carefully in the night, trying to locate the cattle herd by scent and sound since it could not easily be seen. Now and then one of the steers would snort and grumble, like a sleeping man emitting a fatigued snore. Now and then one would invariably rise to its feet to stretch its legs. He would find the herd, he knew. For now, his sense of smell would have to do to bring him closer to the cattle.

Moving carefully across the mostly open ground where only sage and occasional sumac dotted the grassland, he was able to hear the occasional bawl of a restless steer, the bleating of a calf for its mother, and gradually he was able to make out the sleeping herd by starlight. He halted some distance away; he had no wish to startle the cattle, appearing silently out of the night as he was. Moving in behind a clump of head-high purple sage, he began the long wait. A night-rider would appear sooner or later. Sandy would have a chance at the horse he needed.

It was a long while, a long time with his body throbbing and aching, shivering from the dampness his pant legs had absorbed crossing the creek, before a single rider appeared on the dark valley floor. Only now as he planned his attack did Sandy realize how truly stiff he was. Battered, having stood nearly still for a cold hour, his joints were locked, his muscles knotted. He only hoped that his body would respond to what would be his urgent demands. Even were he fully fit this would have been no easy task, but he meant to unseat the rider and steal his pony.

It was that, or quite literally, die trying. There was no way of half-succeeding.

Sandy crouched, bending his knees up and down a few times, trying to loosen them. He debated tucking the pistol away, but decided he had better keep a grip on it even though that would only leave one free hand with which to make his attempt. There was a comfort in gripping the cold weapon tightly, ready to use if necessary.

Only if absolutely necessary. What he was attempting was hazardous enough. A single gunshot at this time of night would stir up the entire valley, send Coyne riders barreling down on him. The end of the game then would likely be Sandy Rivers shot to pieces against the cold earth of foreign soil. The horseman drew nearer.

Sandy waited, his heart racing. The night-herder seemed to be young and slim. His hat was tugged low, shadowing his face in the night. The horse he rode was a fine, well-marked sorrel cutting horse. Sandy could not make out the brand, but it was a matter of indifference to him. The odds were good that it was a Sky Box pony.

The man was so close now that Sandy could hear him softly whistling. Still Sandy waited, still low in a crouch. As the walking horse passed, Sandy leaped from the shelter of the brush, not as smoothly, not as swiftly as he would have liked, and launched himself at the rider, hooking one arm around his waist. The sorrel reared in alarm and, as Sandy's body met the other's, both men were dumped to the ground. The cowboy, who had been expecting none of it, was slow to react as he landed on his face beneath Sandy. Sandy crashed the barrel of his pistol against the rider's skull behind his ear. Sandy tried to do that just hard enough, and held back a little, not wanting to crack the kid's skull.

The cowboy lay still beneath him, sprawled out against the short grass. Before rising, Sandy took the man's gunbelt and holstered pistol. These might come in handy. The sorrel had moved away a little and now stood shaking its head as if annoyed by the games these humans were playing. Sandy moved toward the horse, speaking softly, holding his hand out, and he was able to catch up the sorrel's reins and was allowed to mount. A Winchester repeater rode in a saddle scabbard, Sandy noted with satisfaction.

He rode away swiftly, but silently, angling back toward the creek and the night-shadowed oak grove which would provide concealment while Sandy could come to some determination of what his next move should be.

Run or fight.

That was what his choices came down to. Still uncertain, Sandy glanced eastward and saw the thin arc of the coming moon beginning to lift above the horizon. In an hour there would be no way to conceal his movements. Maybe, he thought, he should just leave the valley and live to fight another day. But where did that leave Corrine? It was a situation of her own making and she seemed to know what she was doing — or thought she did. He could be of no help to her, dead.

It could not be long before the men with the herd noticed that their friend was missing, or until the cowboy himself regained consciousness. Then Sandy would find himself trapped between those behind him and those ahead of him. So for now . . . he laid spurs to the sorrel and the little animal jumped into motion.

Sandy rode due east, into the face of the coming moon, which was now bright yellow, growing fuller as it climbed toward the dark skies. Thinking he heard a shout, he looked back, but no one was following. Not yet.

Half an hour on Sandy had slowed

the horse. The moon was so bright that he squinted into it as he rode, following a vague trail toward the hillrise to the east. There were boulders stacked in jumbles across its crest as well. A place to hide for a while if needed, and he was not so sure that the time for rest was not upon him. It had been long hours since he was able to sleep, and his body was betraying him. His head ached, his left arm was stiff where Coyne's lash had bitten. His shirt was stuck to him, front and back with scabbed blood. Beneath that his assaulted ribs throbbed with a dull, painful reminder of the recent beating.

On top of that he could feel the sorrel faltering slightly. The horse had been ridden long into the night, first by its owner and then by Sandy himself. When the sorrel stumbled clumsily, Sandy made up his mind. It was time to rest, and he guided the sorrel up the slope toward the stacked boulders which were weirdly shadowed now in the moonlight. The place appeared as a crumbling ancient temple where secret alcoves and entranceways led into unknown mountain depths.

A distant movement shook Sandy from his imagery. He thought he had seen — and yes, now he could see a horse and rider coming up fast behind him. He had thought of the jumble of stones as a possible sanctuary, now he saw them as a fortress. No rider coming from that direction could mean him well, and the man on a fresher horse was gaining.

Sandy reached the rocks, dismounting to lead the horse through a narrow gap in the boulders. He paused to look back. The rider was still coming, but he was alone. Once Sandy had position, there was no way a single man could drive him from the rocks. If he intended just to pin Rivers there until help arrived, there was a chance that things might quickly go bad.

Taking the Winchester rifle from its sheath, Sandy fashioned a rough sling for it using his belt and bandanna.

Slinging it over his back, he turned his attention to the rocks surrounding him. Then he began to climb.

The boulders were ancient, time-weathered. At times his fingers would come away, pulling huge sheets of rock free of their faces. His feet found enough purchase, however, to make the climb fairly easy. Twenty feet up he found a flat-topped boulder with good sight lines in all directions, and he dragged himself up to lie prone on it.

He still could not identify horse or rider by this light, at this distance, but he continued to track it with the front bead sight of his rifle. The horse dipped down into a shallow gully Sandy had ridden through and emerged on the near side to slow its dash toward the boulders.

There was no rider on its back.

The man must have dropped off in the gully, and would now be creeping in Sandy's direction, out of his line of sight. Sandy muttered a curse. Climbing the rocks had been of little help to him, but he did not wish to make the climb down, possibly dislodging small rocks and giving his position away.

There was a maze of rocks in the direction of the gully; a cautious stalker would not show himself except in the briefest of moments, and only chance would find Sandy's sights trained at the exact spot. What had seemed like a good thought only minutes ago now seemed utterly foolish. He had trapped himself among the boulders and had no idea where the hunting man might be.

All right, there was no point in brooding about his misfortune or foolishness, he had to get down, recover the sorrel and ride again, ride hard. The stalking man must still be far enough away that it made no difference if Sandy made noise descending. Once he had the sorrel, he would be riding away at speed and the man hunting him would be left behind afoot himself.

So he was thinking as he lowered himself, boots first toward the ground. Halfway down the bluff, the makeshift sling on the rifle came loose and the

Winchester dropped away, clattering off the rocks below. He should have taken more care with the job, but at the time it had seemed more important to get atop the boulders.

Panting, Sandy dropped the last six feet to the ground and looked around frantically for the rifle, but the Winchester was not to be found. It must have fallen into some small crevice or lay hidden in plain sight in the deep shadows at the base of the cliff. Again Sandy muttered a small curse and decided, rifle or not, that it was time to move before the stalking man could catch up with him. He walked rapidly back into the split where he had sent the sorrel he had been riding, carrying his Colt tightly in his right hand. The moon above seemed to follow him, mocking his attempts.

The horse was gone. The moon-shadowed night turned deathly cold.

10

The sorrel must have turned around or found another corridor through the boulders, leading out. It was probably legging its way back toward the herd even now. What was he to do? The only chance seemed to be to emerge from the rocks in the direction through which he had entered. That was the only place where he knew his pursuer not to be. And there was a chance, if slim, of catching up the other man's horse and making good his escape.

That was his thinking. Sandy spun around, holstered his Colt and began jogging toward the opening to the rocky maze. He had made it about twenty yards when the voice reached him from the rocks above.

'Hold it right there, Rivers. The game is over. You lost. I've got my rifle sights trained on your back.'

'What do you want?' Rivers called. He wanted to hear the voice again, to locate the man's position.

'Me? Nothing. Just you or your corpse. If you want to live, shed that Colt and put those hands up nice and high.'

'You know my name,' Sandy said, 'who are you?' But the man would not be goaded into speaking again. Sandy knew roughly where the man was. There was a rock ledge running nearly the length of the entranceway, ten feet or so above the ground. The man had found a way to circle around through the boulders, probably turning Sandy's sorrel horse loose, and clambered up there to wait.

There was a large fallen boulder ten or fifteen feet ahead which would provide shelter, nothing nearer. Sandy would have to out-race the rifle's bullets to the boulder, roll in behind it and prepare to fight it out. None of this seemed possible.

He had hesitated too long and now

he heard the crack of a rifle, and a bullet spanged against the rocky ground only inches from his feet.

'I said shed that pistol, Rivers! My next shot will be in the center of your spine.'

Sandy regretfully lifted the pistol from his holster using his thumb and index finger. He dropped it to the ground. His impulse was to fight back, but he had no chance and at least this way he might live to try it another day.

He heard the man's feet shuffling along the ledge, heard a few small stones and dust trickle down. The rifle shot thundered, flashing brilliantly in the corridor, reflecting off the stone walls as the roar of it echoed down the stony chute.

Then there was the sound of something soft and heavy falling behind him and Sandy turned his head to see a man fall from the ledge and hit the ground, rifle free of his hands.

'Sorry,' a voice from ahead of Sandy said. 'It seems I was a little slow getting here.' The figure of a man separated itself from the gloom of the surrounding shadows and approached.

'Bob!'

'It's me,' Bobo answered. He was wearing a new blue shirt and a black Stetson. His movements as he strode toward Sandy were fluid and easy.

'Looks like you're just about healed up,' Sandy said.

'You ought to see me with my shirt off,' Bob replied. 'It looks like you caught up with Amos Coyne.' Rough fingers examined Sandy's torn shirt and wounded body.

'I did. Who's that over there?' he asked, nodding at the fallen man.

'Looks to be Kent Cox,' Bobo told him.

'Nobody's loss,' Sandy said. 'Tell me, Bob, how'd you find me?'

'Well, I made it back to the Sky Box eventually, still riding that buckskin. The horse didn't go fast nor far in a day, but it plugged along until it got me there. They told me that you and the lady had ridden off together to find

Amos Coyne, which kind of puzzled me.'

'It still puzzles me,' Sandy replied.

'I figured I owed you; besides I'd like to have a talk with Amos Coyne myself. I washed down and had myself treated with carbolic, grabbed a new shirt and saddled Cookie. And here I am.'

'You didn't see Corrine or Coyne, then? Sandy asked.

'There was no way I could have,' Bobo frowned, puzzled for a moment. 'Oh, I see — you and the woman rode the other way, through that town over by the springs. There's another way, Sandy. I came up the south road.' Bobo pointed vaguely.

'So what do we do now?' Sandy asked, leaning against a massive, flat-faced boulder.

'I don't know. What did you have in mind?'

'I was on the run; I thought I might as well run back to Sky Box and get some men to ride back with me.'

'You don't have to do that, Sandy,'

Bobo told him. 'They're already on the way. About two dozen hands.'

'Did you convince them, Bob? Otherwise, how . . . ?'

'That was the plan, Sandy. The girl was to be given a day to try getting the money back from Coyne, then the Sky Box men were to ride. That was planned out by Corrine and Vincent Skye. Skye didn't like it, but Corrine said she could connive the money out of Coyne without a war breaking out.'

'I don't see how she can hope to do it,' Sandy said thoughtfully, 'unless — '

'Unless Amos Coyne realizes the Sky Box is worth a lot more than this little bootstrap ranch of his and Corrine convinces him that he is still at the top of her list as far as husbands go. She, being a woman, and a pretty one, can do that, I would guess.'

Sandy found the idea vaguely troubling, but he had to admit that there was sense to the plan. 'She could have told me what she had in mind,' he complained.

'Maybe,' Bobo agreed uncertainly as he studied Sandy. 'Come on, let's get mounted so we'll be ready for whatever happens.'

'I lost my horse,' Sandy admitted, shamefaced.

'That little sorrel? I found him standing out on the grass like he didn't know which way to go. I tethered him to Cookie's saddle and ground-hitched them.'

'I thank you for this, Bob, you're a life-saver.'

'I couldn't do any less for the man who pulled me back nearly from the grave,' Bob answered.

Together they walked to where Bobo had left the horses. Both still stood there patiently, nibbling at the coarse grass. Their heads came up as the men drew nearer.

'The sorrel's worn down some,' Sandy said. 'He had already put in a full night's work when I took him on a hard ride.'

Bobo nodded, patted Cookie's neck and crouched down, holding the paint pony's reins. 'What do you want to do then, Sandy?'

'I'd guess we should wait for the Sky Box riders, let the ponies rest. My feelings tell me to just ride back and confront Amos Coyne, but that wouldn't be too bright, would it?'

'I'm afraid not,' Bobo said, 'even though I share your feelings. It's more important that we win the war, which we will with twenty men to side us.'

'Coyne still has Corrine!' Sandy said.

'She can take care of herself. Just wait awhile, Sandy. Take the time to breathe and to rest. If you're hungry I've got apples, cheese and bread in my saddle-bags.'

Sandy accepted Bobo's invitation. He took a red apple and cut a slice of cheese with his pocket knife. Then he and Bobo sat together in the cool, moon-bright night, eating companionably.

'They're taking their time getting here,' Sandy said impatiently after a while, looking in the direction of the south trail.

'Don't get nervous on me,' Bobo said with a smile. 'Chuck Durban is heading them up, and he knows what he's doing. My guess is he wants to do any mopping up there is to do after sunrise.'

'I suppose they know what they're doing,' Sandy said, rising from the rock, 'It's just that — '

'I know,' Bobo said, 'it's just that Corrine is still down there and you can do nothing to help her.'

It was at least another hour, with the minutes dragging by, before Sandy heard the sound of hoofbeats approaching. He stood and waited, hands on his hips, looking that way. Eventually the Sky Box riders appeared from out of the night and drew up where Bobo and Sandy stood holding their horses' reins.

'Hello, Bobo,' said their leader, a lanky man wearing a white shirt and a vest.

'Hello, Chuck, we've been waiting for you.'

Sandy muttered a greeting and Chuck Durban fixed narrowed eyes on him. 'Do I know you?' the Sky Box foreman asked.

'We met once.'

'He was a drover on the last drive,' Bobo put in. Durban's expression changed.

'So this is Miss Skye's drover?' he asked with a faint smile which irritated Sandy for a reason he couldn't define.

'This is him,' Bobo answered. 'What have you got planned, Chuck?'

'We mean to hit them and hit them hard. The dead of night is the best time. Most of them will be in their bedrolls. Are you coming with us, Bobo?'

Bobo glanced at Sandy. 'No, Chuck, we'd better try and get to the stone house where Amos Coyne is holed up.'

'Coyne!' Chuck spat the name as if it were poison. 'All right, Bobo. We'll be along to help as soon as we've done what we came to do — wipe these rustlers out.'

'Twenty men won't be able to get him out any better than two,' Sandy told him. 'He's got his house built like a fortress. And besides — '

'Corrine is inside too,' Bobo said.

'I know. But she's smart enough that she may have already made her escape. I'll let you two boys go on and be the heroes. Us? We've got some cattle thieves to shoot.'

After the cowboys had ridden past, leaving them bathed in fine dust, Sandy commented, 'He's a hard man, isn't he?'

'He don't show sentiment easy. All you need to know about Chuck Durban is that given a job, he does it.'

The Sky Box riders were riding, but not rushing, down the long dark slope into the valley. What Sandy had said to Chuck Durban was true enough. Twenty men shooting at the house would accomplish no more than two could. Still, going into battle there was comfort in numbers. Even with Bobo at his side, Sandy felt somehow alone in this battle.

They swung aboard their horses and started riding at an angle toward

Coyne's stone fortress.

What would Coyne do? Try to use Corrine as a bargaining chip, use her as a hostage? Understand that he had been tricked and take it out on her? There was no point in trying to out-think Coyne's evil little mind. As long as he thought that keeping Corrine from harm's way was going to ensure his eventual ownership of the Sky Box, Coyne would not harm the girl.

'Let's have our try,' Bobo said. 'Vincent Skye is waiting for his daughter.'

'What are you talking about, Bob? Didn't you know — Vincent Skye is dead.'

'Well, then, I saw his twin brother yesterday,' Bobo said. 'He had Chuck over to the house to tell him what the plan was. I tagged along and told the old man I was going to go ahead on my own, as even if Coyne caught a lone man on his range it wouldn't give away the raid. I had my excuse for being there ready — I was going to kill Coyne for whipping me. Skye gave me his permission.'

'But he died,' Sandy insisted. 'I was there when they buried him!'

'Couldn't have been,' Bobo said. 'Did you see him rolled into the ground?'

'No, they just planted him while it was still dark. Just Nate Arbuckle, I think, and another man.'

'You really think a loving daughter would have buried Vincent Skye in that manner?'

'It did strike me as kind of . . . cold.'

'And she sent the crippled-up Nate Arbuckle to do the job of burying him?' Bobo was shaking his head. 'No, Sandy. They just told it around that Skye was dead so that when Corrine showed up as a poor helpless orphan — after taking the long way around to give them time to pass the knowledge on to Coyne — he would have already gotten the word and would be licking his lips in anticipation. Probably spouting false sorrow and promising to take care of her.'

'Well, I'll be . . . Why didn't she tell me?' Sandy asked.

'Why would she? If Coyne started questioning you, she wanted to make sure that you believed Skye was dead.'

'This is all a little too cunning for me,' Sandy said. 'Let's quit the talking and get to the doing.'

'Do you have any ideas?' Bobo asked.

'Only one, and we'd better get to the stone house quickly.' Bobo gave Sandy a questioning glance, and he explained his thinking. 'When the shooting starts down in the valley, Coyne is bound to come out to see what's happening. He can't just pull his blanket up over his head, can he?'

'Not hardly. Is he the only one inside — outside of Corrine, I mean?'

'Jordy Cavett and Randall Chandler will be around if they're not inside the house.'

'Probably one inside, one on the porch standing watch,' Bobo suggested.

'That's the way I'd do it,' Sandy answered. 'Come on, Bob, we'd better touch our spurs to these ponies. There's no telling when Chuck Durban will signal his men to rush the herd.'

They were now into the tall scattered pine forest. The moon shone through the high serrated reaches of the trees, making weird patchy shadows on the pine-needle-littered ground. Their horses' hoofs were silent against the cushioning pine needles.

'There it is,' Sandy said, lifting a pointing finger.

'You got better eyes than I do,' Bobo said, squinting down into the valley where finally he was able to make out the squat shape of the stone house.

'I doubt it. I've just been around more recently than you.'

'What are you planning to do?' Bobo asked.

'Find a good position where we can watch the front door and get ready, wait until the guns open up down across the valley. There's bound to be someone on the porch, keeping watch, but we don't want to take a shot at him immediately.

If he is hit, Coyne and whoever else is inside won't come rushing out to see what's happening. If they decided to fort up in that house we could be days, weeks, waiting them out.'

And Corrine would be held inside with them.

'You've got your long gun,' Sandy continued, 'so you find a good shooting spot and keep a hawk eye on the place once the shooting starts.'

'You sound like you won't be waiting here with me,' Bobo said.

'No, I'm going to work my way nearer on foot. If one of them manages to make his break to the open, I'll be waiting to cut him off.'

'I wouldn't want to hit you by accident, Sandy, where will you be?'

'On the far side of the house, of course. I want to keep that stone between me and your shooting. That's the way anyone fleeing will go for the same reason.'

Bobo shook his head a few times before answering. 'All right.' He paused, taking his rifle from its sheath. 'I sure hope this works as planned.'

'It'll work,' Sandy said, swinging down from the sorrel's back. 'It will work.'

Because it had to work. Corrine was still in the clutches of Amos Coyne. She must have had nearly all she could take by now. It was time she was set free. Because if Coyne made his escape he would undoubtedly try taking Corrine with him. She was his most valuable asset, but he could not be allowed to keep her.

On foot Sandy Rivers started down the long grassy slope toward the dark stone stronghold of Amos Coyne.

11

The moon had drifted across the night sky until it was now nearly overhead. It was smaller now, whiter. It peered at Sandy as he wove his way down the slope through the scattered pines. The only man who would be watching for him would be positioned on the other side of the house, on the front porch. They were not worried about Sandy Rivers's return. What could he possibly do? As far as they knew he was still alone, unarmed, and would probably be trying to make his way out of the valley as hurriedly as possible. But they were wrong; Amos Coyne hadn't seen the last of Sandy Rivers yet.

Silently Sandy worked his way behind the stone house, glancing at a corral where Corrine's white mare waited. The other horses were milling around. There was something in the air that night that they did not like. Fortunately, all remained silent as Sandy passed. He continued into the shadows beyond, where the outbuilding stood. He stood behind it and waited, pistol in his hand. He didn't have to wait long. From across the valley a shot rang out, then a dozen more, then what must have been fifty or a hundred. Someone yelled from inside Coyne's house and words were shouted back and forth. Sandy eased up toward the front of the outbuilding where by peering around the corner he could see the front of the big house.

The door to the house was flung open. Rapidly lighted lanterns flared up out of the darkness and sketched a rectangle across the earthen yard. A man lay sprawled, half on, half off the porch. Sandy had not been able to distinguish Bobo's shot from the general uproar, but it was undoubtedly he who had gotten the man from his position on the hill. Sandy thought it must be Jordy Cavett, and was proved right in another minute when Randall

Chandler, shirtless, still strapping on his gunbelt, stuck his head out the door.

A shot from the hillside drove Chandler back inside. Across the valley the shots continued, and Sandy could feel the faint rumble of the ground as the herd of cattle got to their feet, stampeding away from the gunfight. It must have been vast confusion down there with the Coyne men, most roused from their beds, trying to catch up their horses, avoid the panicked cattle and fight back at once. They really had no chance at all, and Chuck Durban hadn't struck Sandy as the type to show much mercy to the men he knew to be traitors to the brand, cattle rustlers and horse-thieves.

Inside the stone house a loud, angry shouting match between Randall Chandler and Coyne continued. Sandy couldn't make out the words with the background of constantly exploding guns, but apparently Coyne was sending Chandler for their horses and Chandler was more than a little reluctant to leave the stone house with all that lead flying.

Where was Corrine? Sandy could not hear her voice. Was Coyne planning to take her with him? Certainly; she held all of his hopes for his future. Even if this plan was falling apart tonight, tomorrow he would still become master of the Sky Box no matter what anyone else wanted. Unless . . . that was as far as Sandy's thoughts went, for at that moment a reluctant Randall Chandler burst from the house and went into a crouch, waving his pistol this way and that before leaping off the porch and dashing directly toward where Sandy was concealed.

'It's time to give it up, Chandler,' Sandy said from the darkness.

Chandler's motion froze. 'What . . . who . . . ?' he asked in panic, searching for a target for his gun.

'I said, just drop it,' Sandy said. Chandler's eyes had adjusted somewhat to the darkness now, enough for him to spot the outline of Sandy Rivers beside the stone outbuilding, and with a little cry of despair in his throat, Chandler raised his pistol and took a wild, desperate shot at Sandy, the bullet ricocheting off the stone face of the building to whine away into the night, joining hundreds of its brothers criss-crossing the moonlit valley.

Sandy had the advantage. He was ready; he had been set and Randall Chandler's figure was plain against the lantern light spilling from the house. He triggered off a .44 round which took Chandler high on the chest on the left side and spun him around to crumple to the earth, his Colt dropping free. Sandy could not be certain that Chandler was dead, but he did not care enough to pause and check. While the door to the house remained open, he meant to get inside.

Running to the porch he leaped up onto its planks — hoping that there was enough light so that Bobo did not mistake him for one of the enemy — and rushed on through the open doorway just as Coyne had decided to slam the door shut.

Heavy oak slammed into Sandy's shoulder, deadening his arm, but he didn't slow his charge. Coyne was fleeing toward a back room. Sandy thought he caught a glimpse of Corrine standing in one corner of the room, but he kept his eyes focused on Coyne, who had now halted and spun, knowing he was not going to have time to escape.

'Coyne!' Sandy shouted hoarsely, but Amos Coyne wasn't taking the time to respond, to hurl words at Sandy Rivers. He reached for the pistol he carried hastily tucked into his belt and began his draw. It was a foolish, desperate move. Sandy's Colt was already in his hand and as Coyne's gun cleared, Sandy shot him. The dark-eyed man staggered backward and came up against an interior wall. He tried to fire his weapon again with the same result.

Sandy fired a second bullet and Coyne, his eyes wide and blank, slid slowly down the wall behind him to an awkward seated position, the white shirt he was wearing developing a spread of crimson across its front.

'Thank God,' Corrine said in a quavering voice, and now Sandy did allow his attention to go to the dark-haired girl who stood trembling in the corner of the room, her fingers raised to her lips as if she would bite off all of her nails. He had never seen Corrine looking so unpoised — or so appealing. He took a step that way as bootsteps thudded against the wood of the porch and Bobo entered, Winchester in hand, his eyes wild. He took in the scene at a glance.

'Too late again,' he said with regret. 'If I couldn't be the man to take him down, I at least wanted to see it done.'

'Sorry, Bob, I should have waited for you,' Sandy said with a grin. Then he walked to the lady in the corner of the room and put his arms around her, holding her tightly while she trembled and looked up at him with moist blue eyes.

'I nearly made a mess of everything,

didn't I?' Corrine asked in a small voice.

'I don't know what you could have done different,' Sandy said in what he hoped was a soothing voice. She took a deep breath and let it out again and her trembling seemed to settle.

'Look at this, Sandy!' Bobo called, his voice loud with residual excitement. Sandy glanced that way, releasing Corrine although he kept one arm around her waist. Outside the shooting had died down and there was now an odd silence like that following the end to a driving rainstorm, The Sky Box men had made short work of Coyne's riders.

'Look,' Bobo repeated. Hanging on a bronze hook on the wall of the stone house was the coiled black bullwhip. Bobo removed it and let it unwind at his feet. His eyes were on the dead body of Amos Coyne. His expression was tight, savage.

'Bob, remember what they say about beating a dead horse — there's no point in it,' Sandy said.

'I know,' Bobo said with a heavy sigh, 'but it sure would've felt good. Say, Sandy, have you still got Coyne's knife?'

Sandy patted his inner vest pocket and nodded. 'I do.'

'Let's have it then,' Bobo said, thrusting out his hand. 'I've got another idea that might make me feel almost as good.' Sandy shrugged and handed over the bone-handled knife. Taking it, Bobo sat down at the rough table in the room's center and began sawing through the woven leather braid of the black-snake whip. Once he had cut it neatly in half he began to smile, but he did not quit working until he had transformed the menacing symbol of Coyne's power into a stack of frayed lengths of leather.

Corrine and Sandy stood watching the obsession of Bobo, understanding it, but a little troubled by it as well. 'There,' Bobo said, finally finished with his handiwork. He rose and went to the still-glowing embers in the stone fireplace and prodded them to life, adding a few small pieces of wood. When the flames rose, Bob began feeding the lengths of leather into the curling flames. The smell was like that around a branding fire, but darker. 'One more thing,' Bobo announced, and as they watched he dropped the knife into the licking flames. Satisfied, Bobo stood with his hands on his hips, watching the red and gold of the flames curl over and destroy all that was left of Amos Coyne's life.

'I'd throw him in, if I could,' Bobo said, nodding at the dead man. Neither Corrine nor Sandy replied. The whole ritual suddenly seemed a little unhealthy.

'Want us to take him outside?' Sandy asked Corrine, looking at Coyne's body.

'Please. If you would,' she answered a little shakily. 'Then you can help me search the house. The money from the sale of the herd has to be hidden in here somewhere.'

Summoning Bobo, each man took a foot and they dragged the remains outside the house and around to the storage shed. Sandy said, 'Those cattle are going to be scattered to hell and back.'

'They will be, but they're bound to come back to the creek for water,' Bobo told him. 'It shouldn't be much trouble rounding them up.'

When they re-entered the house, Corrine was standing near the fireplace, her face beaming as she held up a small canvas bag with a wooden handle for them to see. 'Found it under his bed,' she said with pleasure.

The firelight colored her face prettily. Sandy hesitated and then crossed the room to face her. He did not know if the hug she had given him earlier had been caused by the shock of the moment or if she might have meant something more. He did not know how to broach the subject. Instead he spoke of other matters.

'Bob thinks, and he's right I guess, that the cattle will find their way back to water if not today then tomorrow. So they should be easy to gather. I suppose Chuck Durban will be leaving a few cowhands behind to watch them.'

'He will,' Corrine said. 'I'll talk to

him this morning, whenever they're through mopping up down below. We can't just abandon those steers!'

'No, of course not. They're worth a buck or two,' Sandy agreed.

Corrine looked thoughtful. She turned away, watching the fire burn down. She held the canvas bag still in one of her hands. Her arms were crossed, her head down. Without turning back to face Sandy she said, 'I suppose you would like to be one of the men who stay behind.'

'Why would you suppose that?' Sandy asked with a frown. Corrine still had not turned to face him.

'Well,' she answered, 'that way you'd be a lot closer to that cook over in Bigelow that you wanted to marry.'

Sandy knew that she was joking, but he could not see the point in the gibe. Now Corrine did turn toward him, her blue eyes deep and soft, her dark hair gleaming in the firelight. She placed her free hand on his shoulder and said quite seriously, 'You know, Sandy, I like pups as well. I just don't cook them.'

'Who eats dogs?' a puzzled Bobo asked, staring at the two of them.

Corrine answered, 'No one, Bobo. No one on the Sky Box. The two of us will just get along just fine with one left raw.'

Bobo still had no idea what they were talking about. Then a light glimmered. 'If you two are talking about replacing old Duke, that farmer down south — what was his name? McDougal? — has a brand new litter of black pups. He'd be happy to let you have one, I'd bet. I can go over — '

Bobo quit talking. No one was listening to him anyway, and whatever Corrine and Sandy were saying to each other needed no words.

THE END

Other titles in the
Linford Western Library:

THE DEVIL'S WORK

Paul Bedford

Marshal Rance Toller is locking up a pair of troublemakers when Angie Sutter, a homesteader from a nearby valley, arrives with the news that her husband was murdered that morning. Whilst Rance has qualms about heading out into the frozen wasteland, leaving only an ageing deputy to stand guard, he accompanies Angie to her cabin — to find not only Jacob Sutter's body, but also that of his neighbour, slain by the same weapon. Meanwhile, back at the jailhouse, the deputy is dead and the prisoners gone . . .

REBEL RAIDERS

John Dyson

A gang of former Confederate soldiers is robbing and killing its way across Kansas. Novice lawman Cass Clacy is sent out after them, but what chance does he have of outgunning such experienced fighters? When Sheriff Jim Clarke joins Cass in the chase, his main aim is a share of the reward. Together they penetrate deep into the heart of the Indian Nations, where Cass falls under the spell of the lovely Audrey — but can he save her from the clutches of the dangerous Josiah Baines?